"Are you all right, Elena?" Logan said gently, moving close to her...

"I'm alive," she answered grimly, considering what happened to the victim they just found. "That will have to suffice for the time being."

He held her sturdily in his strong arms. "I'll go along with that."

"Why was she in the woods in the first place?" Elena thought out loud.

"Do you think she went willingly with the person who murdered her?"

"That's a possibility. And it's just as possible she was alone and was killed by a stranger." Either way, it unnerved Elena. "Someone must have been looking for her."

"You'd think so. But that might not have been the case." He released his grip on Elena and said quietly, "We'll get the person behind this."

Elena raised her chin, reading his thoughts. "You think it was The Big Island Killer, don't you...?"

THE BIG ISLAND KILLER

———

R. Barri Flowers

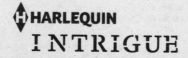

In memory of my beloved mother, Marjah Aljean, an ardent fan
of Harlequin romances, who provided me the tools needed to find
success in my professional and personal lives. To Loraine, the
true love of my life, whose support has been unwavering through
the many years together; and to the loyal fans of my romance,
mystery, suspense and thriller fiction published over the years.
Lastly, a nod goes out to super editors Allison Lyons and
Denise Zaza for the opportunity to lend my literary voice and
creative spirit to the Harlequin Intrigue line.

HARLEQUIN®
INTRIGUE™

Recycling programs
for this product may
not exist in your area.

ISBN-13: 978-1-335-58213-3

The Big Island Killer

Copyright © 2022 by R. Barri Flowers

Harlequin Enterprises ULC
22 Adelaide St. West, 41st Floor
Toronto, Ontario M5H 4E3, Canada
www.Harlequin.com

Printed in U.S.A.

R. Barri Flowers is an award-winning author of crime, thriller, mystery and romance fiction featuring three-dimensional protagonists, riveting plots, unexpected twists and turns, and heart-pounding climaxes. With an expertise in true crime, serial killers and characterizing dangerous offenders, he is perfectly suited for the Harlequin Intrigue line. Chemistry and conflict between the hero and heroine, attention to detail and incorporating the very latest advances in criminal investigations are the cornerstones of his romantic suspense fiction. Discover more on popular social networks and Wikipedia.

Books by R. Barri Flowers

Harlequin Intrigue

Hawaii CI

The Big Island Killer

Chasing the Violet Killer

Visit the Author Profile page at Harlequin.com.

CAST OF CHARACTERS

Logan Ryder—A homicide detective for the Hawaii PD's criminal investigations section, he pursues a violent serial killer dubbed The Big Island Killer. When his former therapist and the woman he's fallen for is targeted, Logan pulls out all the stops to protect her.

Elena Kekona—When the grief counselor and widow takes on the police detective as a client, she never expected to develop feelings for him. But these are jeopardized when he investigates her brother as a possible serial killer. Can they get past this and find love? And does she hold the key to solving the case?

Tommy Nagano—A tour guide and musician who's had run-ins with the law. His world comes crashing down when his girlfriend is murdered and he becomes chief suspect. But is he the ruthless serial killer terrorizing the island?

Aretha Kennedy—The FBI special agent is brought in to assist in capturing The Big Island Killer. Will her experience and dedication to the task lead to bringing the killer to justice?

Shirley Takaki—The forensic scientist is all business when it comes to her job. But can her skills in DNA profiling help crack the serial killer case?

The Big Island Killer—The hard-to-catch killer targets young, attractive Hawaiian women and brutally kills them with different weapons. When Elena comes into the crosshairs, will she be the next one to die?

Prologue

Ever since she was a little girl, Liann Nahuina had rebelled against the conventional order of life and living. Growing up on the Hawaiian island of Oahu, she had been struck by the overreliance on all the things that smacked against doing for yourself, as if there was no other choice. By the time she had re-located to the Big Island of Hawaii two years ago, Liann knew otherwise. Living off the grid suited her. Being self-sufficient and liberating herself from dependency on public utilities and the materialistic world was like a breath of fresh air. Fortunately, she found a like mind in the man who swept her off her feet, and it seemed as if they would be together for-ever, living a minimalistic lifestyle while enjoying the lay of the land.

That was, until disaster struck unexpectedly and her whole world came crashing down like a castle made of sand. The thought gnawed at Liann, like one of her migraine headaches, with regret and what in many respects seemed like an inevitability. Now, once again, she was left to fend for herself and try her best to make the most of a bad situation she was left with. Maybe in the spiritual world, he was still with her, trying to convey in his own way that he wished things had turned out differently. But then, neither of them could have imagined that a common adversary would come between them, resulting in the unthinkable.

Liann pushed aside the disturbing reverie as she approached the place she called home, a small remote cottage on Komohana Street with solar panels and a propane generator. She ran a hand haphazardly through her long, thick dark hair as she entered, stepping onto gray laminate wood flooring. Immediately, as if she was being warned of looming danger, Liann sensed another presence, even though her locked-in brown eyes saw no one. Who would have come there uninvited and made themselves right at home, as if owning the place? One person did occur to her, leaving Liann unsteady on her feet. A feeling of dread permeated throughout her entire slim body like a killer virus.

When she spotted movement to her right, Liann pivoted in that direction. Before she could shield herself, something hard slammed against the side of her face, knocking Liann to the floor, her chin taking the brunt of the contact. Dazed and bloodied, she tried to get up, while attempting to focus on her suspected attacker. She fell short on both counts, as an object came down on her head forcefully, and Liann went out like a light that quickly faded into darkness.

Mercifully, she was unable to feel the subsequent and persistent bludgeoning by a determined and menacing foe, for Liann Nahuina was already dead.

Chapter One

Before they could serve a warrant, the door had burst open and the domestic-violence suspect had opened fire with a semiautomatic handgun, striking Police Detective Hideo Zhang in the face at point-blank range, killing him instantly. That horrific image of his Chinese American partner being gunned down before his very eyes haunted Detective Logan Ryder of the Hawaii Police Department's Area I Operations Bureau, Criminal Investigations Division, on the Big Island. The fact that he then shot and killed the perp before Logan could become his next victim, in what was clearly an ambush, was not enough to shake off the memories of the tragedy almost three months ago. Internal Affairs had cleared him of any wrongdoing in what was self-defense on his part. But even that did little to erase Logan's belief that if he had only acted sooner, or anticipated things beforehand, then maybe Zhang would still be alive today. Instead of leaving his young wife, who was just as torn up about the loss as Logan, a widow.

His mind moved in another equally disturbing direction as he sat up front in a faux-leather chair in a conference room in the Hawaii PD. Located in the *moku* of Hilo, divided into North and South Hilo districts, it was the largest city and county seat in Hawaii County on the Big Island's east coast. It overlooked Hilo Bay, at the base of the active Mauna Loa and dormant Mauna Kea shield volcanoes. Logan folded his arms as he contemplated the murder of two young women in Hilo in the last four months. Both had been the victims of blunt-force trauma to the head. The press had gotten ahead of the investigation in presuming them to be targets of one unsub murderer, dubbed the "Big Island Killer." Though the women had apparently been bludgeoned in different ways, somewhat unusual from the normal predictability of single killers and their modus operandi, Logan was inclined to agree that this was likely the work of a serial killer.

He listened as Police Chief Richard Watanabe spoke about the new task force that had been established to that effect, and included representatives from the Sheriff Division of the State of Hawaii's Department of Public Safety and the FBI. Watanabe, sixty-one and a veteran of the PD in various roles, had been appointed to the position by the Hawaii County Police Commission. "With the unsettling nature of these violent deaths," he said, his forehead creasing below a short head of gray hair with a V-shaped hairline, "it's best to get out in front of this. While the killings thus far all fall within the Area One Operations Bureau jurisdiction, including East Hawaii districts of North and South Hilo, along with Hāmākua and Puna, they could just as easily spread beyond that into Area Two, if we don't stop what seems to be one unsub…" His medium-sized frame seemed to squirm beneath his full police-chief uniform "With that in mind, for those of you who haven't had the pleasure, let me introduce you to the point person for the FBI's participation in the investigation, Special Agent Aretha Kennedy—"

Logan watched as she shook hands with the chief. African American and around his own age of thirty-four, the pretty FBI agent was tall and slender, with big coal eyes and long black locks in a protective hairstyle. Though she was new to them, the PD had worked with the FBI on different cases in the ten years he had been with the force. The Bureau even had a field office on the Big Island, making cooperation between the two law-enforcement agencies that much easier. Rather than view them as adversaries, Logan welcomed any useful input from the FBI, so long as they didn't overstep their bounds for an investigation in which he was the lead investigator.

"The Bureau is glad to be of service to you in any way we can," Aretha said in a pleasant but straightforward voice. "I know that with only two murders currently being investigated in relation to one another, the tendency is not to want to jump the gun in labeling the unsub a serial killer. That's perfectly

understandable. It wasn't all that long ago that fed-
eral law defined serial killings as a minimum of
three murders or more with common features that
were believed to be perpetrated by one or more indi-
viduals." She paused. "Today, the Bureau's National
Center for the Analysis of Violent Crime is listening
to its law-enforcement partners across the country
in constructing a definition of serial murder more
in line with the practicalities and predictabilities in
investigating such crimes in modern times, and the
need to identify as early as possible for the necessary resources and manpower to combat. Toward that
end, the current trend is to look at serial killings as,
at minimum, the murder of at least two people by
one or more perpetrators on different occasions. As
such, I'd say your current unsub qualifies as a serial
killer loose on the Big Island."

Logan nodded with approval, knowing instinc-
tively that whoever had murdered those women was
more likely than not to kill again in sowing the seeds
of serial homicidal behavior. The Bureau, with its
experience in dealing with serial killers, got this.
He would see to it that the task force was fully supportive as they moved forward in solving the case.

"We're all on the same page here, Agent Kennedy," he assured her, having exchanged a few pleas-
antries earlier. "Whatever assistance you can give in
nailing the perp, we'll take it."

"Mahalo, Detective Ryder," she uttered cheerfully.
"I think it's safe to say that whoever we're deal-

ing with here, the unsub's violent tendencies have us all on edge," Detective Ivy Miyamoto said. The newly single and petite but tough-as-nails Japanese American had been with the force for five years. At twenty-nine, she had short brunette hair in a textured pixie cut and small brown eyes. She had picked up the slack in the investigation since Hideo's death, allowing Logan more time to pursue new angles in the case. "It's not a good feeling, especially when having to confront our neighbors, who want this solved in a hurry."

"No one wants that more than I do," Watanabe stressed. "Hopefully, the task force will bring this to a satisfactory ending as soon as possible and we can all go about our business in working other cases." He eyed Logan. "Take it from here, Ryder, and bring us up-to-date on where we're at in the investigation."

"Will do." Standing to his full height of six foot three inches over a solid frame, Logan gave his boss and the FBI agent a nod, then made his way to the large format display. He grabbed the remote off a table, then aimed it at the screen, cut it on and jumped right in. A photograph of an attractive young woman with long, straight dark hair appeared. The sadness in her brown eyes seemed to foretell her fate. "Liann Nahuina, age thirty-one, single and a store clerk. Four months ago, her body was found inside the cottage she lived in alone, off the grid. She was the victim of blunt-force trauma to her face and head. An aluminum baseball bat, identified as the murder weapon, was left behind by the killer as though it was inconsequential once the deed was done." Logan sighed as he considered the nature of the attack. "Unfortunately, we were unable to collect any DNA, fingerprints, or other evidence that could lead us to Ms. Nahuina's killer."

He replaced her image with that of another pretty young woman, this one with blond hair styled in a long shag. "Daryl Renigado, age twenty-six. Three days ago, the registered nurse, recently divorced, was found not far from the Hilo Public Library. She, too, had been bludgeoned to death on and around the head. Her ex-husband, Roy Renigado, a contractor, was questioned, but had a solid alibi and is not considered a suspect in the murder. Outdoor surveillance cameras picked up a tall and slender person of interest wearing a black or dark gray hoodie, dark clothing and dirty white tennis shoes running from the area near where the victim was discovered. Forensics has not as yet been able to give us anything useful from the murder weapon—a wooden mallet left beside the dead woman—apart from the victim's DNA. Or the crime scene itself…"

It was not from lack of trying, Logan knew. He glanced at forensic scientist Shirley Takaki, who headed their crime scene investigation unit and had gone over the scenes of both homicides with a fine-tooth comb, but had come away empty-handed insofar as pointing them in the right direction. The slim, twenty-seven-year-old Pacific Islander had a brown asymmetrical bob and sable eyes, which stared back at him apologetically from her chair. He acknowledged this, but respected the work she did and had no doubt that if this investigation continued, it was only a matter of time before the killer left behind something that would crack the case.

He sucked in a deep breath and said calmly, "So what we have are two women under the age of thirty-two who have generally similar racial and ethnic characteristics of a Hawaiian persuasion, along with being slender, long-haired and attractive. Neither one was sexually assaulted. The manner of death leads us to believe that the killings are related. Or, very likely, the work of one perp.

"If nothing else, the killer is obviously someone full of rage against women," he said with a catch to his voice. "And bold enough to taunt us with these brazen attacks and a clear indication that there will be more to come, unless we can put a stop to it." He gritted his teeth, hating that this was happening under his watch with the pressure building to catch the killer.

Logan presented an illustration of a giant question mark, symbolic of where they presently stood in the investigation. "Who and where is this unsub...?" He let that sink in for a second, then said in clear and precise terms, "It's the duty of everyone in this conference room to work together to come up with the answer. When we have it, we'll be able to put the brakes on the killings before this blows up in our collective faces—" While admittedly being a little overdramatic, he understood that the department expected no less in a case of this degree. Logan felt the same, and didn't wish these types of deaths on anyone. Certainly not if he could help it.

After the meeting ended on a positive note when one of the task-force members mentioned the Merrie Monarch Festival—an annual cultural festival in Hilo next month, with arts and crafts, hula dancing and a grand parade—Logan felt a firm hand on his shoulder. He turned and saw it was Chief Watanabe. "Good presentation," he said tonelessly.

Logan nodded while sensing there was more to come. "I just want to keep things running as smoothly as possible."

"I'm afraid the bumpy roads come with the territory in our line of work."

"I suppose," Logan conceded, still suspicious. *Just what type of bumpy roads are we talking about here?* he asked himself.

"Can I talk with you a sec…?" Watanabe's eyes darted around—they were the only ones left in the room.

"Yeah." He locked eyes with the chief. "What's up?"

Watanabe narrowed his gaze. "How are you doing?"

It was obvious to Logan that he was asking about his mental state in dealing with his partner's murder. "I'm hanging in there," he responded, figuring it was best not to be too high or low in a response.

The chief pondered that for a moment or two, then said, "Losing Hideo Zhang the way you did can be tough to handle, even for someone who has seen his fair share of homicides over the years."

"I won't let it come between me and the job." Logan felt that he'd needed to say it, as though there was an insinuation on the part of his boss.

"I'm sure you want to believe that, but something like this can eat at you like a cancer, no matter how tough you think you are."

Logan jutted his chin. *Where is this going?* he asked himself.

He got his answer when the chief said frankly, "You need to talk to someone, Ryder…"

Logan lifted an eyebrow. "Like a therapist?"

"I was thinking a grief counselor," Watanabe told him.

"Aren't they one and the same?" Logan eyed him defiantly.

"I suppose they are in some ways and not others. A licensed grief counselor specializes in dealing with the pain of loss among other things, such as depression and anxiety." He put a hand again on Logan's shoulder. "I happen to know a good one. Her name is Elena Kekona. I saw her a couple of times last year after my sister had a stroke. It really got to me."

"I remember," Logan said of her illness. He hadn't known about the stroke.

"Elena helped me," Watanabe said thoughtfully. "I think she can help you, too."

"I'm not sure I—" he began, still reluctant to expose his feelings to a total stranger, but Logan was cut off.

"This isn't a suggestion, Ryder." The chief stood his ground. "We need you focused on this Big Island Killer case with a clear head. That can't happen if you're unable to better process the death of Zhang." Watanabe sighed. "I've made an appointment for you to see Ms. Kekona this afternoon. Let me know how it goes…"

On that note, he walked away, and Logan knew from the chief's hard-line demeanor that if he was to continue to take the lead in the investigation, he needed to see this through, begrudgingly or not. Maybe it wasn't such a bad thing if the woman had been able to help the chief deal with his sister's stroke, which she had since recovered from. There would be no such luck here, as Hideo Zhang was gone for good and no amount of therapy was going to bring him back.

An hour later, Logan headed to the grief counselor's office in his department-issued dark sedan. Since Hideo's death, he had been riding solo during a period of adjustment, as the police chief had put it. This was fine by Logan. In fact, if it was up to him, things would stay this way. He preferred his own company since he'd lost the strong presence and dependable friendship of his late partner.

Logan wondered if Elena Kekona could somehow lessen the pain of losing someone he was so close to as he still tried to shake the sorrow he felt like a persistent headache.

The office was located on Waianuenue Avenue. After parking, Logan walked by some swaying *loulu* palm trees that lined the sidewalk and made his way inside and up a flight of stairs to the third-story suite. Having never before sought mental-health counseling, if that's what this was, he wasn't quite sure what to expect. He vowed to keep an open mind. But once he stepped inside, he began to have second thoughts. *Maybe this wasn't such a good idea*, he mused, a natural resistance getting inside his head. He glanced around the reception area, noting its warm ambiance.

Those misgivings swung in the opposite direction the instant Logan's eyes landed on the tall and streamlined gorgeous Hawaiian counselor as she flashed him an incredible wide-mouthed smile beneath big olive-brown-colored eyes and a dainty nose, and uttered smoothly, "Aloha, I'm Elena Kekona."

"Detective Logan Ryder." He saw that her long black hair was styled in a braided updo above a heart-shaped face and imagined what it might look like down and loose. She wore a mixed-color, ruffle-neck shell and brown pencil skirt, and honey-colored slide sandals. Seeing that she had extended her hand to him, he reached out and shook it, immediately sending sparks his way. Did she feel it, too?

Removing her hand from his, Elena said in a sincere manner, "I'm happy to be of service to you, Detective Ryder. Why don't we step into my therapeutic office and talk?"

"Okay," he agreed, following her into what looked more like a comfortable living room, with a cream-colored rustic chenille sofa across from two white grace chairs, separated by a rectangular black coffee table with two potted succulent plants. Sunshine filtered in through a picture window.

"Please, have a seat," she offered, eyeing a grace chair.

Logan sat down and watched as she took the other chair. He suddenly couldn't help but wonder if this—the counselor—was just what he needed to get over the hump regarding his partner's murder.

As a Native Hawaiian, Elena Kekona had always known she wanted to put her master's in psychology from the University of Hawaii at Mānoa to good use. What she hadn't expected was to lose her husband, Errol, a software engineer, to a heart attack three years ago. Dealing with her own unimaginable grief gave Elena a purpose in trying to help others who were going through similar loss in their lives. Becoming a grief counselor in Hilo, where she and Errol had had seven good years together, was a smart decision. Using tried and true methods, such as cognitive behavioral and nature therapy, and newer treatments such as brain-spotting, she had successfully

treated most who had come to her to confront their
issues. In only one instance had her efforts failed
miserably—when a depressed and suicidal man took
his own life, in spite of the therapy and Elena's belief that they had made good progress in getting him
back on track. Though left wondering if there was
more that she could have done to save him, she had
come to the conclusion that some people were simply too far gone in their grief to be brought back
from the brink.

Elena had no reason to believe her newest client
was at such a tipping point in his life as she studied him. In his early thirties, as was she, at thirty-
two, he was tall and certainly as fit as a fiddle, as
the saying went, with regard to physical health. The
detective was above and beyond good-looking and
dripped masculinity, with a square-jawed face featuring hard angles. He had arresting deep-set ocean-
blue eyes beneath slightly crooked thick eyebrows,
an aquiline nose and a crescent-moon-shaped mouth.
His dark hair was cut short on the sides with a layered top and side swept. A short-sleeved blue polo
shirt and black straight-leg trousers fit nicely on his
frame, with black loafers. With that appraisal out of
the way, while ignoring the hot sensations that shot
back at her, Elena turned her attention to the purpose of Logan Ryder's visit. According to his boss,
Police Chief Richard Watanabe, the detective was
struggling to come to terms with the death of his
partner, who'd been killed in the line of duty nearly

three months ago. She recalled hearing about it and could fully relate to the pain experienced not only by the detective, but also by his late fellow detective's widow.

"I understand that you counseled Chief Watanabe a while back," Logan said casually, snapping Elena out of her reverie.

"Yes," she said simply, but knew that was something she shouldn't discuss, even if the chief had sent the detective her way. She gave him a well-meaning smile and said, "If you don't mind, I think it's best that we keep the session on what's troubling you."

Logan nodded, scratching his chin. "Understood."

Good to see he's not fighting me on this in order to detract from his own burden, Elena thought. She gazed at him squarely. "Why don't you tell me why you're here…?"

He paused, as if trying to decide whether he truly wanted to be there or not. Finally, he met her eyes and explained, "Three months ago, I witnessed my partner, Hideo Zhang, being shot to death. Though everyone in law enforcement knows the inherent risks that we face each and every day as part of the job, I haven't been able to let it go. Some, or at least my boss, believe that it's affecting my ability as a homicide detective to perform my duties effectively."

Seemed reasonable to Elena. "And what do you think?" she asked curiously, knowing that denial was often a big part of the problem in coping with loss.

"I think that I'm more than up to the task of doing

what I do for a living," he responded sharply. Logan took a breath. "That being said, I admit that differentiating the death of Hideo from other homicides I've encountered has been daunting at times. Or, to put it another way, I miss my buddy and hate the thought of losing sight of who he was and what he stood for when grappling with new murders that are every bit as grating on the nerves."

"I don't think you'll ever forget him and what he meant to you, Detective," Elena told him, almost wanting to reach over and touch his hand as a show of physical support, to go with emotional understanding. "You have every right to grieve for the loss of your partner. It's a natural means of coping that any of us who have had to deal with the same issue understand all too well."

Logan faced her, thoughtful in his gaze. "Do you mind if I ask who has been lost in your life?"

Elena batted her curly lashes. This usually came up sooner or later, but this early on? She supposed this came with the detective in him. And maybe was his way of sizing her up. "I lost my husband three years ago," she admitted solemnly. "It was quick and not of a criminal nature, but no less traumatic."

"I'm sorry for your loss." He seemed to speak from the heart. She wondered if he was currently married, or ever had been. Somehow it wasn't hard to picture the handsome detective as good marriage material for some lucky woman. Or was she getting ahead of herself in evaluating him in intimate terms?

"Thanks. I've come to accept it as something that neither of us could have prevented." She paused, having wondered more than once if a change in diet, more exercise, or earlier medical intervention might have made the difference. "Anyway, getting back to you, I believe that I can assist you with better coping techniques in dealing with the death of Detective Zhang. This should go a long way toward making you feel whole again and getting on with your life in the ways most important to you, including your career."

He nodded. "I already feel as if something weighty has been lifted from my shoulders."

And very broad shoulders they were, she mused. "I'm glad to hear that." Maybe his treatment wouldn't take so long after all. Elena used the next thirty minutes to further probe into his psyche, as well as what his traumatic experience had taken away from him like a thief in the night, and how it might be restored, short of bringing Hideo Zhang back to life.

Logan appeared to accept everything she brought to the table. But at some point, his mind seemed to wander, even while his eyes were unflinchingly leveled on her. Elena found herself feeling self-conscious and wondering if something about her appearance was embarrassingly off. "Something wrong?" she asked.

Only then did he lower his gaze ponderingly, before lifting again to meet her eyes—this time with a softer edge. "I'm currently working on a serial murder case," he stated tentatively. "Are you familiar with the so-called Big Island Killer...?"

Elena cocked an eyebrow. Who hadn't heard about the murders of two young women, beaten to death, that the press had labeled the work of a single individual they had given the moniker to? Why was he asking? "Yes, I'm familiar with the murders. Not too much that's happening on this island goes unnoticed by its inhabitants."

"Figured as much." Logan lifted his chin. "The victims have, thus far, been in their mid-twenties to early thirties, and had your general features, more or less, and build, with long hair."

"What exactly are you saying?" Elena narrowed her eyes, while reading uncomfortably between the lines.

"Only that, without meaning to frighten you, as long as the killer is still at large, you might want to watch your back," he said in no uncertain terms. "Be aware of your surroundings and if you see or hear anything unusual, it might suggest danger."

Elena took a breath. She certainly hadn't considered that someone out there could be targeting her. Or someone who fit her physical characteristics as a member of the Hawaiian Islands Indigenous Polynesian people. Never mind that Native Hawaiians, such as her, were second cousins to other Pacific Islanders, as well as Filipinos, Puerto Ricans, Portuguese and Japanese, and even Mexicans and Spanish, and thereby opened a wide range of potential female victims who looked alike. Still, living her life in fear in what was supposed to be paradise for what might well be a misleading hypothesis was not an option. She had taken up kickboxing with Errol, mainly for sport, but hadn't remained active in it with him gone. Besides that, she never left home without pepper spray. And since running was one of her favorite pastimes, it was also a way to put some distance between her and a potential assailant. "I'll keep that in mind, Detective," she said coolly, standing. "Thanks for your concern. I'm sure I'll be fine."

"I agree." He grinned crookedly and rose above her, then took a card out of his pants pocket and handed it to her. "All the same, if you find yourself running into any problems with anyone, don't hesitate to call me, day or night—"

Elena glanced at the card that had his work and cell phone numbers. Even if she felt it was unnecessary, she found having access to the good-looking detective reassuring. Did he really mean day or night? The notion of getting to know him outside their occupations was somehow appealing, if not practical, as things stood. "Mahalo," she told him softly.

Chapter Two

More than an hour after he had gone to the counseling session and less than half an hour since Logan had interviewed a coworker of murder victim Daryl Renigado, accompanied by FBI Special Agent Kennedy, he still found himself thinking about Elena Kekona. Apart from her good looks and appealing demeanor, much to his surprise, Logan felt that she had actually helped him in just one session. Or was it more that he was so taken with her that this made everything else she was selling seem like something he was more than happy to buy? Either way, his mind was certainly more open to the notion of needing someone to help him in addressing Hideo's death than before. More uncomfortable was the belief that Elena fit the general profile of the victims of the Big Island Killer, in terms of being part of the ethnic Polynesian group on the island. Whether she believed this or not, the therapist was not safe so long as the unsub was free to pick and choose women who looked or carried themselves like her. And for that reason, if no other, Logan welcomed the upcoming encore meeting as a chance to get a better handle on the woman and her ability to protect herself from an unseen but deadly enemy.

He glanced at the FBI agent in the passenger seat—she was busy texting someone. *Business or personal?* he wondered. Maybe, like him, she had no personal life. His had ended, romantically speaking, more than a decade ago, when the supposed love of his life had decided it was just a one-way street. He could only hope the day would still come when love worked both ways for keeps. Had Elena given up on love and all its magical properties with her late husband no longer in the picture?

"So I imagine you've come across other serial killers like the one we're chasing?" Logan got the agent's attention, mindful of the FBI's updated view on what constituted a serial killer in the modern era, with two murders and counting.

Aretha shut off her phone. "Yeah, there's been others the Bureau has gone after that were prone to one degree or another to bludgeoning their victims to death, as opposed to strangling, shooting, torturing, poisoning, or whatever," she pointed out matter-of-factly. "Infamous names that come to mind as perpetrators of murders mostly by way of blunt-force trauma include Ted Bundy, Terry Rasmussen and Gerald Gallego, to name a few."

"Figured as much." Logan considered some of the familiar serial slayers, keeping his eyes on the road as he drove down Kapiolani Street, wondering what made such killers tick. How were they largely able to seem perfectly normal on the outside and so capable of such brutality whenever the dark spirit moved them from within? "Is there any method or madness to the time between one murder and another? Or, in other words, does the fact that the first two murders attributed to the Big Island Killer occurred nearly four months apart buy us some time?"

"Not necessarily." She sighed. "The time frame may be more a reflection of opportunity or circumstances that prevented the killer from killing sooner after the first kill than anything. If you ask me, the Big Island Killer is more likely than not to pick up the pace now that the unsub has two killings in the bag. Making it even more critical for us to identify and apprehend."

"Could the killings have been stalled because the perp simply was lying in wait to find a suitable target, no matter how long it took?" Logan asked, pondering out loud.

"Yeah, it's possible. But since it's not all that difficult to find beautiful women of Hawaiian descent or similar on the Big Island to kill, the urge to do so, or not, may be less about homing in on the perfect victim than other triggers, such as stress, along with influences like alcohol and/or drugs."

"Okay." He wondered what some of those additional triggers might be. Hatred? Lust? Prejudice? Revenge? Or something else? Whichever way he sliced it, Logan still couldn't help but believe that the unsub was on a mission, and that, for whatever reason, Hawaiian women in particular appeared to be singled out for victimization. Meaning his counselor, Elena Kekona, even if not necessarily being targeted, per se, was still vulnerable to attack.

After arriving at police headquarters, Logan caught up with Detective Ivy Miyamoto, who was seated at her desk in the middle of the large room with cubicles. She faced him as he walked up to her. "Hey," he said inquiringly.

"We've released the still shots and surveillance video of the person of interest in the murder of Daryl Renigado to the media and all law enforcement on the island," Ivy said, a look of optimism in her eyes. "Though the suspect is moving away from the camera, meaning we can't see the face, there's still the body shape and clothing that, hopefully, will get the ball rolling in leading to an opportunity to talk to this individual, if not make an arrest."

"Yeah, that would make our job a little easier, if someone recognizes the person in the video and comes forward." Logan was optimistic, but was realistic, too. This was hardly a clear-cut road map to solving this case. If, in fact, the suspect running from the crime scene was the killer and not a passerby who'd panicked. "Too bad the video is pretty grainy and doesn't exactly give us any facial characteristics or hair style and color of the person in it," he muttered. "What is clear is that it's an obvious attempt to disguise oneself with the hoodie and dark clothing. If I didn't know better, I might think that the suspect even planned to be captured on the video, as if to toy with us, while knowing it would give an incomplete picture for us to grapple with."

Ivy twisted her lips. "I doubt the unsub is that clever. But we'll see if the video and picture yield any results." She shuffled a stack of papers and looked up at him. "What did you come up with on the victim's coworker?"

"Not much," Logan admitted. "According to the woman, Candace Piena, also a nurse at the Hilo Medical Center, Ms. Renigado left work at approximately six p.m. to drop some books off at the library. There was no indication that she was being followed or otherwise in fear for her life."

Ivy frowned. "Oh, well—we'll keep digging."

"Yeah." Logan headed to his own desk, while wondering when the killer might strike again, assuming they didn't get to the perp first. He was cut off by Chief Watanabe, who asked, without diffidence, "How'd it go with Elena Kekona?"

"Pretty good, actually," he confessed. "You were right—I think the counselor might be able to help me overcome whatever issues I'm having with Hideo's death. In fact, I have another appointment with her tomorrow."

"Glad to hear that." A pleased look brightened the chief's face. "You can thank me later."

Logan grinned. "Will do." His thoughts turned

to Elena, as he wondered how things would go for
the wilderness therapy session she had planned. She
didn't exactly strike him as someone who was necessarily as much at home with nature as not. But then
again, he didn't know what he didn't know, and may
have been selling her short. Maybe she would give
him the opportunity to discover more about her beyond that she counseled troubled people like him.

ELENA STEPPED INSIDE the Prince Kūhiō Plaza, the Big
Island of Hawaii's largest enclosed shopping mall,
feeling the air-conditioning hit her face after the
humid outside air. She made her way past stores,
restaurants and a movie theater, then reached an
open area, where a children's hula dance group was
performing as free entertainment for tourists and
locals alike. Elena smiled as she watched the young-
sters dance to the sound of the song, "Hawaiian Hula
Eyes," before she turned to the trio playing the music.
Or, more specifically, her brother, Tommy Nagano,
who was playing a ukulele. It was a part-time gig to
supplement his full-time job as a tour guide.

At twenty-nine, Tommy was three years her ju-
nior. Tall, lean and handsome, he had their father's
brown-gray eyes and short black hair in a tight fade
cut, with a stubble beard on his round face. He was
wearing his usual attire of an orange Hawaiian print
shirt, relaxed-fit jeans and sneakers. In his youth,
Tommy had had a few run-ins with the law for minor
infractions. Elena was thankful he seemed to have

gotten that out of his system. With their parents dead and no steady relationships, they only had each other to lean on, as was traditional in the Hawaiian culture when it came to family.

When the show went on break, Tommy came over to her with a big grin on his face. "Hey, sis."

She gave him a little hug. "Thought I'd check in on you after work before heading home."

"What did you think?"

"As always, I think you're great," she admitted, as a sister would. "The kids really seem comfortable with their routines, which are made easier because of the music."

"I was thinking the same thing." He ran a hand over his head thoughtfully. "You know, you look more and more like Mom with each passing day."

Elena blushed, knowing that many, herself included, considered their mother—or *makuahine*, in Hawaiian—beautiful. "I'll take that as a compliment."

"Would it be anything else?" He chuckled evenly.

She smiled and glanced at his fellow band member who played the keyboard—she was an attractive and shapely twentysomething Hawaiian with long raven hair in voluminous waves. "Who's the new girl?"

"Her name's Kat," he said simply.

Elena wondered how long it would be before he hooked up with her, knowing that he seemed to have a new bedmate every other day. "She's pretty."

"And she also has a boyfriend," Tommy pointed out, as if that had ever stopped him from going after someone who captured his fancy. Elena sometimes wished she could be as free in romance. The better part of her knew she was a one-man woman. Since Errol's death, there had been no one else. She was ready to move on, but only with the right man. For some reason, Detective Logan Ryder entered her head. She wondered if Tommy could ever be all right with her dating a cop, given his negative view toward police officers. Maybe if he kept an open mind...and she did as well—

"Well, the show's about to start again," Tommy said, breaking her reverie. "I'd better head back."

"All right." She gave him a hug. "Catch you later."

In the parking lot, Elena got in her blue Subaru Outback, started it and took off. A few miles later, she was pulling into the private driveway of her two-story, two-bedroom custom redwood house on Laimana Street. It had a porte-cochere entry and French door. Stepping inside and onto a travertine-tile floor, she took in the spacious interior, with its open concept and floor-to-ceiling windows, great room with vaulted ceiling, proper dining area, gourmet kitchen that had solid wooden textured cabinets, granite counters and a farmhouse sink. There was a mixture of modern- and retro-style furnishings and transitional ceiling fans throughout the home. The wraparound lanai opened to tropical landscaping that included banana, lemon, papaya and tangerine fruit trees, along with plumeria and coconut palm trees, and a Balinese two-story gazebo. Located not far from the Wailuku River, Elena had purchased the place with her husband. It was supposed to be their dream home, but had ended up being a place where she lived alone. A detached *ohana* unit that was accessible by way of its own private, gated lava-rock-walled entry yard was being rented out to Tommy.

After kicking off her shoes, Elena went to the kitchen and poured herself a glass of white wine. While tasting it, she found herself pondering the not-so-subtle warning by Detective Ryder.

You might want to watch your back.

Could she really find herself coming face-to-face with this so-called Big Island Killer? Or was she getting carried away at suddenly being paranoid over the notion that someone could try to take away the very life she'd built while destroying any future she might have? Elena sipped her wine as a more proper perspective crept in. She understood that the detective was merely doing his job in telling her to be on the lookout for danger, and she very much appreciated it. But there was really no cause to be alarmed. At home, she had Tommy around the corner much of the time, should trouble come calling. And elsewhere, she was around enough people in public places to make it unlikely that a murderer would single her out.

With those calming thoughts, Elena finished the wine, then tried to decide what to have for dinner.

THE NEXT DAY, she was up bright and early looking forward to her session with Logan Ryder, perhaps more than she should have been. After all, it wasn't like this was a date. He was her client for now, and needed a bit more of a push to get past his partner's death. And never mind that she had an earlier client before their 10:00 a.m. outing. The fact that she'd chosen to meet him at Wailuku River State Park instead of her office was more about using ecotherapy as a more relaxing environment to tackle his issues. Anything else was being premature, in spite of feeling a connection with the detective, even if she was unsure what it meant. If anything.

After dressing in a pink boatneck top and green twill shorts, worn with casual sneakers and sunscreen, Elena put her hair in a low ponytail and headed to work. When the time came to rendezvous with the detective, he was already waiting for her at the sixteen-acre park, just west of downtown Hilo.

"Hey." His voice was soothing and his grin infectious.

"Aloha." She tried to maintain an even keel in spite of his strong presence, if only for professional integrity.

"Thought I'd arrive a bit early to soak it all in."

Elena smiled, studying him. His clothing was similar to what he'd worn yesterday and was just as form-fitting on his muscular body. Only this time, he was wearing black athletic sneakers. "In case you're wondering about the location, I like to bring clients to one of my favorite places on the island as a therapeutic way to balance nature with delving into emotions."

"Works for me," Logan assured her, a comment that Elena took to heart in continuing the journey into self-discovery.

"Let's walk," she said. As they did so, Elena ignored the sheer force of his manly presence and focused on the purpose of the visit. "Why don't you tell me more about your partner. What was Hideo Zhang like?"

"Where do I start?" Logan pondered thoughtfully. "On the job, he was dedicated, but didn't take it so seriously that he forgot what was truly important in life."

"Which was?" Elena asked.

"His wife and marriage," the detective said matter-of-factly. "Hideo understood that their love would always be front and center, with his career needing to take a back seat to family and everything it meant to him."

Elena choked up at hearing the heartfelt words. Neither she nor Errol ever lost sight of those principles. While the extended family never came, the intent was always there before it was so cruelly taken away. She wondered where Logan stood when it came to family and work. "Are you or have you ever been married, Detective Ryder?" she asked, hoping he didn't consider this too intrusive.

Logan rubbed his chin. "I was married once a

long time ago to a botanist named Gemma. Didn't work out. Seems like she couldn't handle being married to a cop." His gaze fell. "I blame myself for that, at least to some extent. I didn't always put her first, the way I should have. But I can't go back. If there's a next time, I'll do it the right way—"

"Good for you." She admired his honesty and assumed he was currently on the market. Or was she reading him wrong? They reached the 80-foot Rainbow Falls just in time to see a rainbow created by the combination of mist and sunlight.

"It's beautiful," Logan remarked, peering at the falls.

"Yes, I agree." Legend had it that the cave below the waterfall was home to the ancient Hawaiian goddess, Hina. Elena gazed at the scenery in awe, sensing the setting was accomplishing its purpose in softening him with the therapy.

Their shoulders brushed as Logan commented, "Hideo was an adventurer. He loved to hike, scuba dive, ride horses, you name it."

"Sounds like he led a full life," she said, feeling the electricity pass between them like a bolt of lightning.

"Yeah, I think he did."

"As such, that's all any of us can ask for in the short time we're here."

"You're right." Logan flashed her a sideways grin. "Good way of looking at it."

"Grief has a way of making us draw on the worst

rather than the best in coping with loss," Elena pointed out. "I'd like to think that your partner understood that on some level."

Logan nodded, as if this idea had begun to take shape with him, as well. They began to walk again in silence. Oddly, Elena saw this as part of the process. The quietness broken only by the calming sounds of nature allowed a person time to reflect internally. They reached Boiling Pots, a sequence of large, terraced pools that connected by way of underground currents, with bubbling, rolling water, that gave the appearance of boiling.

"I was thinking that Hideo's widow, Leilani, has had a difficult time as well coming to terms with his death," Logan said, gazing at the water. "I believe she could benefit from your counsel."

"I'd be happy to talk with her," Elena said, quick to offer her services.

"I'll bring it up to Leilani." He turned toward Elena. "If we're almost done, do you want to grab a bite to eat? I missed breakfast and could use something in the system before heading back to work."

She, too, felt hungry, while at the same time having butterflies in her stomach at the thought of spending more time together. Was it a good idea? Or not? "What did you have in mind?" she asked cautiously.

Ten minutes later, she had followed his vehicle to the Tastes of Hilo Food Truck on Kilauea Avenue, where Elena ordered a grilled-cheese sandwich and Logan a club sandwich.

"So, are you any closer to solving the Big Island Killer case?" Elena had decided to ask the detective out of curiosity, and maybe a little uneasiness about the murderer being on the loose, since he had brought it up the day before.

"Wish I could say we were." Logan used a napkin to wipe mayonnaise from the corner of his mouth. "Unfortunately, the investigation is still ongoing and the killer still at large."

"I see." She bit tentatively into the sandwich, wishing he'd had better news on that front.

His eyebrows knitted. "Why? Have you seen anything or anyone that was suspicious?"

"Not that I can recall," she said thankfully. "But don't worry, Detective, I'm keeping my eyes open for any signs of trouble."

"Glad to hear it." His cheeks rose. "By the way, call me Logan if you like. I'm not on duty right now, as such."

"All right, Logan." She smiled. "As long as you call me Elena, even as a grief counselor."

"Elena, it is." He finished off the sandwich. "And when do we meet again for the next session…?"

"Actually, we don't," she replied, surprising herself by saying it.

Logan lifted an eyebrow, apparently puzzled by her statement. "Excuse me?"

As much as she wanted to continue to see him,

Elena felt she needed to be honest about it as a professional. "I don't really see a need," she said sincerely. "Usually, I only need to counsel a person for one to two sessions—unless there is a need for more. In your case, I believe I have done my job by giving you several things to work with in coping with your partner's death. The rest is really up to you."

"I understand," he muttered.

"Do you?" She gave him a questioning look. The last thing she wanted was for them to part on bad terms. But she wouldn't have felt right taking his money and time as an excuse to continue spending time with him. Didn't he get that?

"Of course." Logan finally put a smile on his handsome face. "I'll do my best to cope using the pointers you gave me." He paused. "Guess I'd better head back to work now."

"Me, too." Elena made herself smile back, while wondering if it was a mistake to watch him walk away. Or was it the right choice for the right reasons? *Am I really ready to have a love life again?* she asked herself. Maybe it was time to move on. With any luck their paths might cross again. If so, Elena only hoped it wasn't just because she needed Logan's help as a crime victim, but because she wanted the chance to explore where she and the police detective could go on a more personal level.

Chapter Three

Why didn't you just ask her out already? Logan chided himself, a beer in hand and a frown on his face that next afternoon. He was standing on the covered lanai at the back of his two-story house, surrounded by mature hibiscus, plumeria and Fiji fan palm trees. His home sat on a four-acre parcel of rural land, bordering the Waiākea Forest Reserve. His eyes strained to see the Pacific Ocean beyond. He had asked himself the same question maybe a thousand times since yesterday, when Elena had released him from his compulsory counseling. Though pleased to be given his walking papers, insofar as being fit for the job as a homicide detective, even if the grief of losing his partner still lingered somewhat, Logan hadn't been quite ready to break contact with the striking counselor. But something had held him back from pursuing her on a more personal level. And he knew what that something was. The truth was he wasn't sure if she was up to dating a cop and all that it encompassed any more than his ex was. And he wasn't ready to risk getting his heart broken again. Maybe he never would be.

Logan took another sip of the beer before stepping back inside the country-style, three-bedroom home in a gated community on Kulaloa Road. He had purchased the completely fenced property a year ago. On the main floor, the living room was spacious with a coffered ceiling. A formal dining room led into a large kitchen with a breakfast bar and stainless-steel appliances. There was engineered hardwood flooring and picture windows throughout. Tropical-style furniture and decor made the place feel like home, with brushed-nickel ceiling fans in every room. But even with that, Logan knew that he wanted someone to share it with someday before it could ever be complete. He imagined that Elena could be that person. Maybe if they had met under other circumstances, at a different time and place…

The chiming of his cell phone caused Logan to lose his train of thought. Lifting the phone from his pocket, he saw that the caller was Detective Ivy Miyamoto. He connected her. "Hey."

"I just reviewed surveillance video from the Aloha Hardware Store on Keawe Street in Hilo," Ivy said. "The day before Daryl Renigado was killed, a man identified through his credit card as Glenn Sewell was seen purchasing a wooden mallet and latex gloves. It could be coincidental, but it's worth checking out."

"I agree," Logan told her. "I'll meet you there."

"Okay." She texted him the address.

Though they were hardly at the point of probable cause, much less ready to slap on the cuffs, for now Logan definitely considered Sewell a person of interest in the death of Daryl Renigado and, by extension, Liann Nahuina. Checking to make sure his Glock 17 semiautomatic pistol was still safely tucked away in the duty holster attached to his belt, in case it was needed, Logan headed out.

Ten minutes later, he pulled up behind Ivy's official vehicle outside a small, two-story plantation house on Hualilili Street in South Hilo. Logan got out and met the detective halfway between their cars. "See anything?" he asked her.

"No one's gone in or out." Ivy tucked her hair behind an ear. "But since the Range Rover Sport in the driveway is registered to Sewell, I'm assuming he's inside."

That was good enough for Logan, so he said, "Let's go."

They crossed the street and walked up to the door, where Logan rang the bell. He was tense, as always, when confronting a potential suspect in a murder investigation. At the same time, he understood it was a process and that not everyone they encountered was an offender. This time around remained to be seen. When the door opened, a twentysomething Latina female with midlength feathered blond hair was standing there. "Yes…"

Logan flashed his badge. "Detective Ryder of the

Hawaii PD," he told her, and added, "And Detective Miyamoto. We'd like to speak to Glenn Sewell."

She looked noticeably uncomfortable. "What has he done?"

"Maybe nothing," Ivy said ambiguously. "What's your name?"

"Julie," she said succinctly.

"Julie, is he here?"

"Yes." She paused. "Wait just a moment."

"Actually, I think it would be best if we waited inside," Logan insisted, wanting Sewell to feel their presence, should he want to make a run for it.

Julie nodded reluctantly, stepping aside as they moved into a small living room that was traditionally furnished. Ill at ease, she yelled upstairs, "Glenn, the police are here. Can you come down?"

Momentarily, a muscular man in his early forties, with a short blond faux-hawk haircut, came lumbering down the stairs. He looked warily from Logan to Ivy, before settling on Logan. "What's going on?"

Logan studied him, deducing he wasn't carrying a piece. "We need to ask you a few questions."

"About what?"

Ivy stepped forward. "A purchase you made six days ago at the Aloha Hardware Store," she said bluntly. "Surveillance video picked you up buying a pair of latex gloves and a wooden mallet."

"So…" He wrinkled his bulbous nose. "Is that a crime?"

"Only if used to commit a crime." She peered at

Sewell suspiciously. "The day after your purchase, someone using a wooden mallet bludgeoned Daryl Renigado to death, leaving the murder weapon behind. Mind telling us where you were the evening of March eighteenth?"

"I was at home with my girlfriend, Julie." Sewell chewed on his lower lip. "Ask her."

"We will. Right now," Ivy told him, "We'd like to see the mallet you bought…and the latex gloves."

The suspect ran a hand across his mouth, seemingly breathing a sigh of relief. "No problem. I didn't use the mallet to kill anyone. Come with me…" He led them out the back door to a workshop behind the house. A wooden mallet was on a steel workbench. "It's been right there since the day I bought it," he said. "See for yourself."

Logan and Ivy examined the mallet without touching it. It looked new and was obviously not the one used to murder someone. Still, Logan considered that the suspect could have simply replaced one mallet with another. "Where are the latex gloves you bought?" he asked him, knowing they could potentially contain DNA from the crime.

"Right here," Julie answered, having followed them into the workshop. She held up the gloves. "Glenn bought them for me. I needed them for my gardening. I can show you…"

Logan recalled the tropical garden they'd passed before entering the workshop. "That won't be necessary." He glanced at Ivy, who was in agreement, as both of them realized that they were likely barking up the wrong tree here. Still, to be on the safe side, Logan asked Julie to verify that Sewell was with her on the day in question, which she did. For now, the detectives had no solid reason to believe otherwise. "We won't take up any more of your time," Logan told the couple, as he and Ivy saw themselves out.

When back at her car, Ivy groaned, "Looks like a big nothing burger."

Logan didn't exactly see it that way. "We both know we have to go through a few detours to get to the finish line."

"I suppose," she muttered in agreement.

Logan blinked, thoughtful. "See you later."

Ivy cocked an eyebrow. "Where are you going?"

"To the cemetery," he stated, leaving it at that as he headed to his vehicle.

A short while later, Logan was at the Hilo Memorial Park, making his way across the damp grass until he came to the grave site of Hideo Zhang. He observed someone already there, as expected, with flowers lying against his headstone. The woman never looked his way, as though too caught up in the moment to hear him coming.

"Leilani…" Logan called out softly.

In her midthirties, Leilani Zhang was small-boned and attractive, with delicate features on an oval face, hazel eyes and long dark hair with blond highlights, styled in zigzag curls. Like her late husband, Leilani was Chinese American. She turned his way and just stared, as if in a trance, then uttered, "Logan—"

"Figured you'd be here," he told her, knowing it had been exactly three months to the day since Hideo had been gunned down. She started to bawl and Logan took her in his sturdy arms.

"I miss him so much," Leilani spluttered, crying into his shirt.

"I know you do." Logan fought hard to keep his own emotions in check. "So do I." He thought about how Elena had helped him better process things and believed she could do the same for Leilani.

Half an hour later, after paying their respects to the fallen detective, Logan followed his widow back to her town house on Kumukoa Street in central Hilo. The carpeted, roomy place had natural lighting, cathedral ceilings and a warm ambiance, with sleek contemporary furnishings. The only thing missing was the usually upbeat presence of Hideo. Instead, Leilani was left only with a Tonkinese cat named Mona to keep her company. Along with the memories of Hideo.

Logan shared those as she made them a cup of *māmaki*—Hawaiian herbal tea. After taking a sip, he said to her casually, "I've been to see a grief counselor in dealing with Hideo's passing."

Leilani looked up from her cup, as they stood in the U-shaped kitchen. Mona sat on a rattan stool, quietly observing them. "Really?"

"Yes. Her name is Elena Kekona. She's helped me

in ways I didn't think possible." He paused to gauge Leilani's reaction, knowing her to be a private person when it came to dealing with her emotions.

"Maybe I should go to see her," she suggested.

Logan nodded. "Yeah, I think that's a good idea. I can call her and set it up."

"Mahalo." A weak smile played on her lips.

While he hoped Elena could work her magic on Hideo's widow, Logan also looked forward to having an excuse to reconnect with the attractive counselor. Not to mention check on her, hoping to keep her out of harm's way with a serial killer on the loose.

ELENA GREETED LEILANI ZHANG as she stepped into the office, after Logan had called to make an appointment for her. "I'm so glad you came," Elena said.

"I nearly chickened out," Leilani confessed. "But since you came highly recommended by Logan, I figured that maybe there is hope for me in trying to carry on without my husband there to hold my hand."

"There's definitely hope for you, Leilani." Elena realized this was precisely her own mindset after losing Errol. Her entire world seemed to crash in on her at that point, making it seem like there was no more tomorrow worth pursuing. Thankfully, she'd been able to get over that difficult hurdle and get to the other side, realizing there was still a whole world out there that she deserved to be a part of. The same was true for Leilani. And Logan, too, for that matter.

Elena led her latest client to the therapy room,

where she did everything possible to make her feel at home. That was always the key to reaching a level of trust that was good for both sides in addressing the grief that could make or break a person if it wasn't harnessed properly.

"I understand that you also lost your husband early in life," Leilani said evenly.

"Yes, three years ago." Elena realized that it was still painful to talk about. But she had to, if she hoped to get Leilani to do the same. "Heart attack. It came on very suddenly and…that was it. I never saw it coming. I doubt that he did, either."

"That must have been devastating to you." Leilani fluttered her lashes. "I mean, it isn't exactly something you can prepare for, is it?"

"No, it isn't," Elena admitted, no matter how strong she tried to be and realistic in the knowledge that someday they would all leave this earth. But the focus should not be on her life and loss, as she pivoted back toward the detective's widow. "Why don't you tell me about what you've been going through these past months since you lost your husband."

Elena listened as Leilani went through the typical emotional roller coaster experienced by survivors, empathizing with her every step of the way. How could she not feel for Leilani in losing someone you had given everything to?

"It's been tough," Leilani concluded, finishing on a sigh.

"It's perfectly normal to feel the effects of grieving," Elena pointed out to her. "What's key is to be able to keep things in a proper perspective."

Leilani frowned. "How do I do that?"

Elena answered by giving her tips on positive reinforcement, compartmentalizing and thinking in terms of moving on, as her loved one would have undoubtedly wanted. Leilani seemed amenable to these techniques, giving Elena confidence that she would be able to get past the death of Hideo Zhang and make her own life count for something.

When the session had neared an end, Leilani brought up the Big Island Killer investigation that was currently underway. "I hope they catch the person soon," she remarked.

"You and me both." Elena shuddered at the thought of being the victim of a serial killer. "Log—Detective Ryder seems determined to solve the case."

"I know." Leilani nodded thoughtfully. "Hideo was working with Logan when the first victim was killed." She sighed. "I only wish he had lived at least long enough to be around when an arrest was made and we could all breathe easily again on the island."

Elena found herself reaching out and touching her hand. "Maybe part of him is still alive in the spirit of Hawaii, as a sort of angel on Detective Ryder's shoulder in carrying on in law enforcement without him."

"I think you're right." Leilani offered her a tender smile. "I'm glad Logan talked me into visiting you."

"So am I." Elena imagined that she would be a great person to hang out with beyond the therapy sessions, with their similar storylines. Along with the common link in Logan.

After she had seen the client out, Elena called him to let him know the session went well and that Leilani had made an appointment for a second visit. He seemed pleased, thanking her for, as he put it, "coming to her rescue." Though flattered, Elena saw this as her calling and was always happy to help those in need.

Then, abruptly, Logan said in a level voice, "Do you want to get together for a drink?"

She didn't need any time at all to think about it, as Elena was ecstatic to spend time with him in a nontherapeutic way. "I'd love to."

That was all he needed to suggest they meet at a place not far from her office in an hour. She was all in, even if a part of Elena wondered exactly what that meant, in terms of expectations. Or should mean in terms of where they might go from there, when it came to possibly starting something with the gorgeous and dedicated police detective.

ADMITTEDLY, LOGAN FELT like he was sixteen again, looking forward to his first date, as he waited at Veronica's Lounge on Kanoelehua Avenue for Elena's arrival. The difference was, while those high-school dates were largely forgettable, there was nothing about the gorgeous counselor that he wouldn't always remember. Whether anything could come out of this remained to be seen. He would take it one step at a time and see how things played out.

The moment she walked in the door, Logan's heart skipped a beat. Apart from her pleasing appearance overall, Elena had her long hair down for the first time, making her all the more appealing to him. "Hey," he greeted her.

"Hey." She walked up to him and smiled.

"Let's get a table." Logan followed closely behind her as they found a spot and sat. After she had met with Leilani, his partner's widow had called him and had nothing but good things to say about Elena. Seemed as though the two women might actually come out of this as friends. Maybe the type of friendship he and Hideo had. Or, Logan mused, the kind he could have with Elena himself, assuming it never reached that of a romantic nature. "What would you like to drink?" he asked her.

"I'll have a Lava Flow," Elena told him.

"Good choice." Logan ordered it and went with a Kiwi Colada cocktail for himself. He found he wanted to know everything about her. Or at least anything relevant in shaping her into the person she was. "Do you have family on the Big Island?" he asked after the drinks had come.

"Yes, my brother, Tommy, lives in Hilo," she said. "He's currently renting an *ohana* on my property, separate from the main house."

"And your parents?"

"They passed away some years ago." Elena tasted

her drink and Logan immediately regretted bringing them up, knowing that she would then think about her late husband. "I believe they're still together in some spiritual realm, which is a good thing."

"I agree." He leaned back in his chair.

"What about your family?" She met his eyes.

"My parents split up when I was very young," he recalled. "My mother is still alive and living in Northern California, the Bay Area, where I grew up. A few years ago, I reconnected with my father before he died of liver disease."

"Sorry to hear that," she said.

Logan was thoughtful. "Yeah. At least we were able to form some sort of relationship toward the end."

Elena regarded him curiously. "Any siblings?"

"No siblings," he responded with regret, believing that it might have made his life easier if he had brothers or sisters to lean on during difficult times.

"How did you end up on the Big Island?"

"To make a long story short, I was recruited by the Hawaii Police Department to fill an opening, after working with the California Department of Justice's Human Trafficking and Sexual Predator Apprehension Team. Guess I had become burned out at that point in investigating trafficking cases, often involving the sexual exploitation of women and children, and decided I needed to move in a different direction."

Elena took another sip of her drink. "Any regrets?"

Reading her mind, Logan supposed she wondered if going after human traffickers and sexual predators in favor of serial killers and other homicide-related offenders was much of a trade-off. He saw both as equally heinous in nature, but the incidence was much greater with the former than the latter. Rather than delve too deeply into those dynamics, instead, he told her earnestly, while appreciating the view across the table, "From where I'm sitting at this moment, I'd have to say no regrets whatsoever."

She blushed and uttered, "You're smooth, I'll give you that, in skillfully dodging the question."

He grinned, enjoying this easygoing communication between them. Where else could it lead? "On balance, having the opportunity to live and work in Hawaii, even if it's less than utopia, I'd gladly do it over again."

"I'm glad you made that choice, Logan," Elena said sincerely, meeting his eyes.

"So am I." In that moment, it seemed like an ideal time to kiss her—those soft lips that seemed ever inviting. Leaning his face toward her, Logan watched for a reaction that told him they weren't on the same wavelength. Seeing no indication otherwise, he went in for the kiss. It was everything he expected—sweet, sensual and intoxicating. Only when his cell phone chimed did he grudgingly pull away.

He removed the phone from his pocket, glanced at the caller ID and told Elena, "I need to get this."

"Please do," she said understandingly.

Before he even put the phone to his ear, Logan sensed that he would not like what he heard. He listened, anyway, as Ivy spoke in a near frantic tone. Afterward, he hung up and looked gloomily at Elena, and said, "The body of a young woman has been found." He paused, almost hating to say this, considering the concerns he still had for the safety of the grief counselor and not wanting to unnerve her. But there was no denying the truth or sparing her what she needed to hear. "It appears that the Big Island Killer has struck again."

Chapter Four

Logan took the coastal drive down Kalanianaole Avenue toward Onekahakaha Beach Park, where the victim had been discovered. From his brief chat with Ivy Miyamoto, the woman appeared to be Hawaiian, and fell into the mid-twenties to early thirties age group, similar to the others targeted by the Big Island Killer. This made it all the more disturbing to Logan, especially now that he was starting to feel something for Elena Kekona, who matched the general description of the dead women. But he couldn't exactly ask Elena, even with the kiss that had seemed to up things a notch between them, to put her life on hold until they caught the unsub. Even if he could, he doubted she would listen. Not that he could blame her. He just didn't have enough to go on at this point to start making demands on her, or any other woman who could potentially be in the crosshairs of a killer.

All I can do right now is try to catch the perp and end this nightmare for Hilo and the Big Island once and for all, Logan mused with determination, as he turned onto Onekahakaha Road, soon coming to the parking lot. After getting out of the vehicle, he made his way to where the activity was, with crime-scene tape cordoning off the area where the body had been found. He flashed his identification to a thin officer with a French crop, who allowed him through, before Logan rendezvoused with Ivy and FBI Agent Aretha Kennedy, who were both wearing nitrile gloves.

"Sorry to have to get you down here," Ivy told him. "But it looks like our serial killer is back at it."

"When duty calls, the job comes first." Logan frowned. He'd known it was just a matter of time. After all, serial killers never seemed to stop—until they were taken down.

"If this is our unsub, that makes three," Aretha said, as if to validate their categorizing of the previous two murders as the work of a serial slayer.

"Point taken." Logan gritted his teeth. "Where is she…?"

"Right this way," Ivy answered, leading them past crime-scene investigators at work collecting possible evidence, and other law enforcement officers who were actively engaged in the investigation. They came to a section of grass beneath a clump of evergreen trees. "That's how she was found…"

Logan eyed the female lying on her side in a pool of blood, as though positioned as such. Nice looking, or would have been were she still alive, she had long, multilayered brown hair, was slender and around five-five or five-six, he deduced. The victim was fully clothed in a purple tie-front T-shirt, gray terry shorts and black running sneakers. Her vacant russet-colored eyes were open, as if for a final look at her killer. Logan grimaced at the unsettling image and could only imagine what had gone through her head as she was being killed. "Who is she?" he asked.

"According to the driver's license found in a handbag near the body," Aretha responded, "the victim's name is Yancy Otani, age twenty-five. It looks like she was jogging before being accosted by the unsub." The agent muttered an expletive. "The killer probably caught her from behind while she was still on the move."

"It was certainly a brazen attack," Ivy remarked, raising her eyebrows. "A witness reportedly saw a tall person wearing a dark hoodie and dark clothing running away from the scene."

"Same as the last victim," Logan muttered thoughtfully. "The unsub is getting reckless—making the attacker even more dangerous."

"Tell me about it," forensic analyst Shirley Takaki said dramatically as she approached the group, wearing protective equipment. "The perp really went to town on the victim." With gloved hands, she was holding a large evidence bag containing what looked to be a big, bloodstained lava rock. "We think this is the murder weapon."

Logan smirked, troubled that the unsub seemed capable of using all manner of weapons to attack the victims, as though to keep them off balance. What would be next? "Hopefully, you'll come up with some DNA we can use," he declared pessimistically.

Shirley made a humming sound. "If it's there, I'll find it."

"I know you will." Logan had no doubt that she and her team welcomed the challenge of putting their scientific expertise to the test with each criminal investigation. But would that be enough to catch a crafty killer?

"Hey, get over here, Campanella," she barked at Martin Campanella, the thirty-year-old crime-scene-and-evidence photographer who was new to the team. His predecessor, Joan Gonzalez, had quit after getting in with the Bureau of Alcohol, Tobacco, Firearms and Explosives.

Campanella, tall and lanky with crimson hair in a topknot, walked over with camera in hand and said, almost apologetically, "I'll try not to get in the way."

"I think it's more the other way around," Logan stated aptly, as they made room for him to photograph the deceased and surrounding potential evidence.

"Only a matter of time before the unsub slips up," Ivy said, removing her gloves.

"In this instance, time is our enemy," Logan indicated sourly, taking in the surroundings for what was supposed to be a family-friendly park and not a place of murder and mayhem. "The more time goes by, the greater likelihood the killer will strike again and again."

"I've got agents fanning out with your officers," Aretha reported, "looking for anyone who fits the description or otherwise may know something."

"Maybe we'll get lucky." Logan wanted to believe this, knowing that sometimes a good break was all they needed to find the perp and solve the case. More likely, they would need good old-fashioned legwork, modern technology and forensics to arrest the culprit.

"Whatever it takes to end this nightmare," said the forensic pathologist, Dr. Bert Swanson, who came to claim the body. The sixtysomething subspecialist in pathology was of medium build, with gray hair in a comb-over style and a salt-and-pepper ducktail beard. "This trend is something none of us, least of all me, want to keep putting up with as the bodies start to pile up."

"Tell me about it." Logan curled his lip cynically. He thought about Elena and dreaded even the possibility of her suffering the same fate. He watched as Swanson crouched down and lifted the deceased's severely damaged head with his gloved hands and manipulated it a bit, as if a rag doll. "Did she die the same way as the others?" Logan asked anxiously, realizing it was possible that it was a different killer, in spite of the similarities in the manner of death.

"My preliminary finding is that she succumbed from the injuries sustained from the solid blows to the back of her head," the pathologist said tonelessly. "I'll be able to give you a more definitive answer when I complete the autopsy, first thing in the morning."

"See you then," Logan said, if only to confirm what they all pretty much knew. Yancy Otani had been bludgeoned to death the same way as the other victims of the Big Island Killer. Meaning they had their work cut out for them if they were to make any significant headway in identifying the unsub and getting the person off the street before anyone else was added to the collection of murdered women.

IT HAD BEEN a couple of hours since Logan had left Elena at Veronica's Lounge, after learning that someone else had been murdered. She was admittedly spooked by the whole notion of a serial killer in their midst. This frightening reality undercut the kiss she shared with the man, nice as it was. Logan's tender lips were amazing. It left her longing for more. Whether they would get the opportunity to build upon that kiss or not, she couldn't say. Was she really up for getting involved with a police detective, especially at this time? Would his job always come first? Would hers?

As she grappled with those thoughts from the comfort of her great room, Elena leaned back on the burgundy velvet sofa and rested her arm against the wingback shoulder. She had checked the local news and not gotten much information about the body discovered at Onekahakaha Beach Park, other than it was a young woman, who appeared to have been the victim of foul play. Was she another victim of the Big Island Killer? More than a little curious, Elena wondered if it would be appropriate to ask Logan directly about the investigation. *Given his concern about my safety, and a vested interest in the case as a resident of Hilo, where the murders were occurring, I say yes*, she told herself. Lifting the cell phone she had been holding, Elena called the detective before she lost her nerve.

He picked up on the second ring. "Hey, I was just thinking about you," he spoke in an ultrasexy voice, as though picking up where they left off at the lounge.

"Really?" She knew the same was true in reverse.

"Yes, I just wanted to make sure you made it home safe and sound." His more serious tone brought Elena back down to earth.

"I did," she assured him. "That's kind of why I'm calling. I was hoping you could update me on the body found—if only for my peace of mind."

She sensed some hesitancy on the part of the detective, as if he wasn't in a position to share sensitive information. But then he said straightforwardly, "A young woman is dead—murdered in a manner similar to the others victimized by a serial killer. I'm sorry to have to lay this on you, but you have a right to know—especially since the victim, like the others, bears a strong resemblance to you. Not to say any could have passed as your identical twin, and all were a bit younger, with varying heights. However, what they share in common with you besides being attractive and long-haired with a slender frame, is that all are Hawaiian, as far as we could determine."

Elena sucked in a deep breath while mulling over his weighty words. "What do you think that means?" she asked, putting herself into the proverbial shoes of the victims.

"Not sure at the moment," he told her frankly. "I'm guessing the perp has some particular beef against Native Hawaiian women and is targeting them."

She tried to imagine what that beef might be. Why them and not others? Was there a method to the killer's ostensible madness? Who knew what went on in the minds of psychopaths? Elena thought, assuming the killer was operating with such a mental disorder and not fueled purely by hatred. "I'll do my best to be on guard," she said, sensing he was thinking that very thing. Even then, she wasn't under any illusion that she could ever be totally safe from a determined foe. No matter the safety measures taken. Still, she had no desire to be a sitting target for a killer, any more than the next woman living on the island. "I do have my brother around for added protection," she stated. "Tommy's not exactly a bodybuilder, but he's fairly fit and protective in his own way."

"That's good to know," Logan said in a level tone of voice. "But should he or your self-protection not be enough, I'm just a phone call or car drive away."

"I appreciate that, Logan." The kiss between them flashed in Elena's head. She wondered if it was still registering with him, too. Or had the investigation already made it little more than a distant memory. "Well, I should let you get back to it. Thanks for the update, sad as it was to hear."

"I think it's best to be up front on things like this," he insisted defensively. "Knowing what you're up against can sometimes make all the difference in the world."

"I agree." How could she not, all things considered? "Talk to you later," she told him and hung up.

After taking a moment to reflect on Logan, the murders, the kiss and her own reality, Elena figured she would pop over to see Tommy, feeling in need of some company and maybe reassurance that everything would be all right. She grabbed her keys and left the house, locking the door behind her, and headed through the open gate and down the lava-rock entry yard. She spotted Tommy's black Volkswagen Atlas in the driveway before arriving at his front door. Elena listened in to see if he might have a woman inside, or otherwise be entertaining friends. Hearing nothing, she rang the bell.

When the door opened, Tommy appeared in dark jogging attire and gym shoes. His hair was damp, as though he'd been working out. "Hey," he said in his usual easy tone, studying her.

"You busy?" she asked.

"Nah. Was just fooling around a bit in the exercise room. Everything all right?"

"Yes, I'm fine." Or at least as fine as could be expected after learning that someone like her had been found beaten to death.

Tommy tilted his head. "Come on in."

The inside was a two-bedroom guesthouse, with an en suite and full kitchen. Tommy had converted one of the rooms into his own home gym. The style of the *ohana* was much like the main house architecturally, with an open feel and travertine-tile flooring, along with modern vintage furnishings.

"Want something to drink?" Tommy asked, even as he headed to the refrigerator and took out two cans of strawberry guava juice. Elena took one from him and sat on a dark blue retro sofa, then watched as he flopped onto a wide brown barrel chair. He looked at her and asked perceptively, "So, what's up?"

She sighed and opened the juice. "Did you hear that another woman was killed in Hilo?"

He cocked an eyebrow. "Really?"

"Her body was found at Onekahakaha Beach Park," she told him. "She'd been murdered like the other women purported to be victims of the Big Island Killer."

"Damn. Sorry to hear that." Tommy took a gulp of his strawberry guava. "Did they arrest the killer?"

"Not that I've heard." Elena paused, thinking about Logan. Was there any chance that he and Tommy would get along, if it came down to that? "I understand that the police and FBI are pulling out all the stops in trying to get to the bottom of this and put someone away. Until such time, truthfully, it's got me feeling a little unnerved."

He gazed at her with concern. "Why, has someone been threatening you?"

"No," she responded quickly.

"Do you suspect someone of being this killer...?" His voice raised an octave.

"No. But apparently all the victims look basically like me." Elena tried to process that in her own head.

"Says who?" he asked point-blank.

Without bringing Logan into the conversation, she responded evasively, "It's in the news. I've seen their pictures. The killer is targeting pretty young women of my racial and ethnic persuasion. It doesn't take a rocket scientist to realize that I could be next on his list, at least in theory."

"I doubt that." Tommy waved his hand nonchalantly. "No one's coming after you, sis."

"You sound pretty confident about that." Her lashes fluttered. "I'm no safer from victimization than any other native Hawaiian female on the island. Not while the killer remains at large."

He frowned. "So, what, you think that all young Hawaiian women are suddenly at the mercy of some psycho?"

Elena considered Logan's views on the subject. As a lead investigator on the case, she had a feeling that his observations and instincts were probably spot on.

"I wish I could say otherwise," she told her brother. "I'd just like to err on the side of caution until this is over." She paused while regarding him. "Having you nearby is comforting…at least when I'm at home."

Tommy's features eased. "I don't think you have anything to worry about, but since you are clearly worried, you can count on me to be there in a snap if you sense any trouble, wherever you happen to be."

"Mahalo." She smiled at him, glad to know he had her back. Just as she knew that Logan did. But would either be able to protect her from a determined killer? Or would that ultimately fall on her?

"In the meantime, just keep your guard up," he said with earnest. "Killers usually like to catch victims unprepared and aren't too interested in those who are observant and actually willing to fight back."

Elena laughed. "Looks like someone has been watching too many episodes of *Hawaii Five-O*," she teased him.

"Just telling it as I see it." Tommy drank some more of his juice. "Honestly, sis, what I think you really need is a man in your life."

"Oh, really?" Her eyes popped wide. This should be interesting.

"Yeah. Errol's been gone long enough. Time for you to get on with your life. I know you're a strong independent woman and all, but c'mon. There's someone else out there for you to share and share alike. I'm just saying…"

"Look who's talking," she challenged him, even if the thought of sharing her life with someone special was appealing. A man like Logan would probably fit the bill, she imagined, if they were ever to give it a go. "Coming from a guy who seems to have a different woman on his arm every other week."

Tommy grinned crookedly. "What can I tell you, I'm just trying to find the right one to give it a go with."

"When you do, let me know." Elena gave him a sarcastic look and sipped her drink.

"Ditto," he told her, before getting to his feet. "I'll walk you back to the main house."

"Okay." Though she felt fairly safe in the upscale neighborhood, and her own residence in particular, Elena welcomed the offer. But could anyone ever feel safe enough in the current environment in Hilo, in spite of Logan and his colleagues being hot on the trail of a serial killer?

Once inside her home, Elena locked the door behind her, while Tommy headed back to the *ohana*, claiming he planned to make an early night of it for an early start with a guided tour the next day. Given his penchant for partying sometimes into the wee hours of the morning, she was suspicious of just what his plans were for the evening.

As for herself, Elena took a quick shower before bed, having eaten earlier. After putting on a chemise nightgown and applying moisturizer to her face, she walked into the master suite, with its rustic furnishings and large windows. After climbing onto the panel platform bed, she tried reading a few chapters of a novel she had started, but could not seem to focus on anything but the latest poor woman who had been murdered, ending any dreams she had for the future. Elena imagined the grief her loved ones would experience, having been on that side of the equation in dealing with such loss. Turning her thoughts to Logan, Elena wondered what type of stress he was going through in trying to solve the case, over and beyond having to deal with the recent death of his partner. She was sure Logan was strong enough to adjust accordingly. Elena was not as confident where it concerned becoming romantically involved with the detective, in spite of the potency of a single kiss and its rippling effect on her body. Could he handle a relationship while pursuing a serial killer? And beyond? Could she? Or were any possibilities between them doomed to failure, even as she tried to move on with the hope of finding love as a widow, as Errol would surely have wanted. These disquieting questions lingered in her mind as Elena fell asleep.

Chapter Five

Even though it was ten at night and he dreaded having to be the bearer of bad news as he arrived at his destination, Logan would not shirk from his duties as a lead homicide detective. Unfortunately, this included being assigned to informing loved ones about those who passed away. In the case of Yancy Otani, that sad news had to be delivered by phone half an hour earlier, given that the murder victim's parents lived in Sacramento, California—the family had relocated there a few years ago from the island of Maui. He had few answers to give them, apart from the obvious. As soon as the autopsy was completed, the body would be released to a funeral home and any arrangements for transport could be made then. For now, the victim's remains were still evidence in a murder investigation, one which Logan hoped would lead them to a killer.

Among Yancy Otani's belongings was her University of Hawaii at Hilo campus ID card. Her parents verified that she was an out-of-state graduate student seeking a master's of science in tropical conservation biology and environmental science and resided in an apartment on Aupuni Street. Logan knocked on the sixth-story door. Opening it was a thin young woman in her early twenties with blue eyes and light auburn hair in a graduated style with curtain bangs. She was clad in a pink peplum top and denim shorts. Flashing his badge, he said in an equable voice, "Hi, I'm Detective Ryder of the Hawaii Police Department. And you are…?"

"Shailene Leclerc."

"Are you Yancy Otani's roommate?"

"Yeah." Her eyes narrowed. "Did something happen to her?"

"Mind if I step inside for a minute?" Logan asked, hoping not to have to discuss the matter in the hallway.

She stepped aside and he walked into a small living room with neatly arranged country furniture. "Where's Yancy?" Shailene persisted.

Always the hardest part, Logan thought. But there was no getting around it. Especially when he still needed to question the roommate about the victim. "I'm sorry to say that Ms. Otani is dead—"

"Dead?" The color seemed to drain from Shailene's face. "How…?"

"She was murdered." Logan paused. "Her body was found at Onekahakaha Beach Park."

Shailene's shoulders slumped. "It was that Big Island Killer, wasn't it?"

"The investigation is still underway." He didn't want to be too presumptuous before it was confirmed. "I can assure you that whoever did this will be brought to justice." Logan hoped the words didn't come across as hollow. Especially since he had said the same thing to family and friends of the other victims, more or less. But he still believed this to be true, if he had anything to do with it.

"Have you gotten in touch with Yancy's parents?" Shailene's eyes watered.

"Yes," he told her with regret. "Naturally, they're broken up by the news." How could they not be? Logan considered how he felt when witnessing the murder of his partner. And how Elena felt in losing her husband. These things would be tough for anyone to take. That included the victim's roommate. "I need to ask you a few questions…"

Shailene wiped away tears. "Okay."

"We believe that Yancy was jogging in the park when she was attacked. Does she often jog there?" He noted that it was a few miles between the apartment complex and Onekahakaha Beach Park.

"Yes, she jogged there a few times a week—usually after her shift was over at the Pizza Isle on Punahoa Street, where she worked part-time."

Logan considered that someone who knew her routine, including an employee at the restaurant, could have followed her to the park and killed her. "Was Yancy seeing anyone?"

"No," Shailene said swiftly. "Between school,

work and staying in shape, there wasn't much time for dating."

"Did she have any enemies, stalkers, or anyone she seemed to be concerned about?" Logan asked routinely, but still needed to know for the record.

"Not that I can recall. She got along well with everyone." Shailene's lower lip quivered. "I can't believe she's gone...just like that."

"I understand what you're going through," he told her. More than she knew. "Look, if you need to talk to someone, I know a grief counselor who could help you deal with this." When she seemed to be open to the possibility, he gave her Elena's name and contact info, knowing that her office welcomed anyone coping with loss and other traumas. Finally, Logan asked Shailene gingerly, "Do you think you're up to IDing the body?" Though they were fairly confident that the murdered victim was Yancy Otani, this would make it official, given the distance and time it would take for her parents to get there.

Though she looked to be barely holding up on wobbly knees, Shailene agreed to accompany him to the morgue. Another punch in the gut for Logan in the course of a murder investigation. After the mission was successful, unfortunately, he dropped the victim's roommate back off at her apartment and called Ivy as he drove off, putting her on speaker. "Yancy Otani worked at the Pizza Isle restaurant. She left her vehicle, a red Hyundai Sonata, there while she went jogging at the park. We need to have it dusted for prints and see if any DNA collected will point a finger at someone."

"I'll get the CSI unit over there right away," Ivy told him.

"I'm heading over there now to speak with employees and check out surveillance video," Logan said. "Whoever killed her may have been at the restaurant and trailed her to the park, before catching her off guard."

"I'll meet you there." Ivy sighed. "The rising body count is starting to get to me. The unsub is almost daring us for a showdown."

"We're more than up to the task, believe me." To suggest otherwise would be handing the perp a victory. That wasn't going to happen, as far as Logan was concerned. He doubted Ivy felt any different, in spite of the frustration he heard in her voice.

"I do," she stated flatly. "One person—even such as this serial monster—can't come out ahead of an entire task force that's pretty pissed off right now."

"Couldn't agree more." Indeed, they were all fully committed at the Hawaii PD, along with their partners in law enforcement, to working overtime to bring the unsub to justice. No matter how long it took. As if he needed any more reasons to that effect, Logan had one, anyway. Elena Kekona. Yes, he knew that her brother was around for her to lean on right now and help safeguard her from danger. But was he really equipped to take on a serial killer if push came to shove? For that matter, was Elena even safe while at work? What would prevent the unsub, if the perp believed she fit the profile of his other victims, from spotting her by chance and going on the attack when Elena least expected it? The mere possibility of losing her shook Logan to the core, even though he and the counselor had yet to even go out on a proper date. Much less become involved in something akin to a real relationship.

Calm down, Logan ordered himself, having disconnected from Ivy as he neared the restaurant. *Don't freak out prematurely.* Elena was a grown woman and smart enough to take precautions to ensure her own safety, wherever she happened to plant her feet. As much as he wanted to be her protector with a murderer at large, Logan didn't want to do more harm than good in being worried about Elena. The last thing he wanted was to come across as more of a hardheaded cop than a man who had genuine feelings for her, but not obsessively so. His best bet at this point was to take it slow and let things play out naturally. At least where it concerned Elena. There was no slowing down in the hunt for the unsub. The sooner they put an end to the perp's reign of terror on the Big Island, the sooner Logan could concentrate more fully on the woman who was unknowingly making his heart patter.

STUDYING THE SURVEILLANCE VIDEO, Logan saw Yancy Otani leave the restaurant on foot, en route to Onekahakaha Beach Park. She gave no indication of anxiety or belief that she was being followed before she disappeared from view. No one appeared to be following her. "Let's back it up and watch again," he told the manager, Karen Foxworth, who was in her midthirties with orange hair in a diagonal fringe cut.

"Sure thing," she said, and rewound the video.

"Doesn't seem like anyone's on her tail," Ivy stated tonelessly.

Logan frowned. "Maybe the unsub met up with her later." Or not. "Rewind until a couple of minutes before Yancy comes into view." The manager complied. "Stop!" Logan ordered when he spotted some movement in a corner of the screen. "There's a person standing by some bushes—"

"Yeah, you're right," Ivy said. "They seem to be going out of their way to stay inconspicuous."

Logan felt the same thing. "Can you zoom in on the person?"

"Yes, I can do that." Karen brought the image closer. The person was tall and slender, wearing dark clothes and a hoodie. Logan couldn't make out the face or hair, covered in shadows.

"Looks like our person of interest," Ivy remarked.

"It does, doesn't it?" Logan concurred, locking in on the suspect.

"You think he went after Yancy and killed her?" Karen's mouth hung open in fury.

"That's what we intend to find out," Logan responded tersely. "Does that person look familiar at all?" He eyed the manager, thinking it could be an employee. Or a regular patron.

She peered at the image for a long moment. "I don't recognize them. Sorry. Maybe one of my staff can help you identify the person."

Logan pursed his lips. "Why don't you fast-forward the video past when Yancy disappears from the screen."

"Okay." Karen did as he asked.

"Stop!" Logan snapped as he spotted the person in the hoodie begin to move in the direction the victim had gone. "The unsub's following Yancy, presumably in the process of tracking her down in the park and murdering her."

Ivy muttered an expletive. "We'll see if we can match this up with other surveillance video that leads to the park. Could give us a better description of who we're looking at."

"Do it," Logan told her. "Maybe some eyewitnesses can help us ID the unsub." The better part of him believed they would unmask this perp eventually, surveillance video or not. But could they do so before the killer decided to strike again?

Eight hours later, after a mostly sleepless night, where his head was filled with thoughts of the Big Island Killer, the unsub's victims and Elena, not necessarily in that order, Logan got dressed and settled on coffee with a little cream and a bagel for breakfast. Then he headed for the forensic pathologist's office to get the official autopsy report on the death of Yancy Otani.

"I was expecting you," Bert Swanson said the moment Logan stepped into his domain. The office itself was spacious with modern furnishings and equipment.

Not wanting to beat around the bush, Logan asked, "So what are we looking at on the death of Yancy Otani?"

Swanson scratched the hair on his chin, then responded authoritatively, "Just as I suspected, Ms. Otani died of the injuries sustained due to blunt-force trauma."

"Can you be a bit more specific?" Logan had no desire to hear the gruesome details. But as a homicide detective, he needed to believe they were talking about the same killer here.

"Of course. The victim's death was caused by blunt trauma to the back of her head and neck. The killer likely pummeled her repeatedly with the lava rock that I, along with your forensics department, determined to be the weapon used to kill Ms. Otani. It dealt something akin to a crushing blow that the poor woman simply had no chance to survive."

Logan furrowed his brow, the thought of such a violent ending playing on his emotions. "In your professional opinion, do you think she was killed by the same unsub we believe bludgeoned to death Liann Nahuina and Daryl Renigado?"

Swanson took a breath and locked eyes with

Logan. "That's ultimately your call, Detective, but based on the autopsy results from all three homicides—illustrating severe trauma with blunt force—I'd have to say that we're almost certainly looking at a serial killer with a thirst for extremely vicious behavior."

Logan nodded. "I expected as much," he muttered, wondering if he would have felt any better had there been three separate killers. The fact that they were looking for a single individual did, if nothing else, allow them to focus their investigation in one direction.

"Unless you want us to keep doing this song and dance," the pathologist warned with a catch to his voice, "I highly recommend that you and your team find this killer and stop the madness."

"I hear you." Logan gave him a sincere salute, meant to show that they truly were on the same page in knowing what needed to be done if the female residents on the Big Island were ever going to be able to rest easily again. That included Elena, whom he was still keen on getting to know much better, even in the midst of a serial-killer investigation. He wondered if she was up to having dinner at his place. Or would that be more than she was ready for at this point?

ELENA HAD A restless sleep before morning came. She had a disturbing dream in which the Big Island Killer was chasing her in the dark of night. Just as the faceless, hooded killer was about to descend upon her maniacally, Logan seemed to come out of nowhere to her rescue, stopping the villain cold. Afterward, Logan scooped her in his arms, kissed her passionately and, she supposed, they lived happily ever after. Awakening, Elena blushed at that last thought, which was purely speculation. She only knew that the detective saved the day in her nightmare and she was eternally grateful for that, even if it was only a dream that Logan would never know about in the real world.

Guess I really let the latest murdered woman get to me, Elena thought, reclaiming her equilibrium and sense of reality, before climbing out of bed. She needed to keep a proper perspective as she began her day. Last thing she needed was for an unidentified serial killer to both invade her dreams and drive her crazy with fear while awake. Wasn't that what all serial killers wanted at the end of the day, to get into the heads of vulnerable women like those being targeted, giving the offenders a psychological boost over and beyond the killings?

Declaring that she wouldn't allow herself to become a victim, Elena freshened up and dressed, put her hair in a French twist updo, had cereal and black coffee for breakfast, and was out the door for work. She noted that Tommy's car was gone, indicating that he had already left for the Hilo tour he was guiding this morning. She was glad they got to talk last night, as they didn't have heart-to-hearts nearly as often as they did when they were younger.

After getting into her own vehicle, Elena started it

and took off. At 9:00 a.m., she had her first session of the day with a woman named Marybeth Monaghan. In her early thirties, she was tall and lean, yet big-boned. Her jet-black hair was in a pixie bob cut, surrounding an angular face and blue eyes behind geometric-shaped beige eyeglasses. She was wearing a floral print midi dress and brown ankle-strap sandals.

"Aloha," Elena greeted her with a smile.

"Thanks for seeing me," the woman said politely.

"How can I help you, Ms. Monaghan?"

"Please, call me Marybeth," she insisted. "Ms. Monaghan was how they always referred to my mother, who was a single mom, until she passed away recently..."

Elena showed appropriate sympathy. "I'm so sorry to hear that."

"It's the reason I'm here." Marybeth's voice shook. "Guess I just needed someone to talk to about it."

"I understand. I'm happy to offer my services." Elena recalled when she lost her own mother and then her father. Both deaths were devastating, taking a piece of her away forever. Obviously, Marybeth was going through much of the same journey of grief and transitioning to life afterward. After the payment had been taken care of, Elena said, "Why don't we go into my therapy room and talk?"

She led the way and sat across from the new client. "How did your mother die?"

Marybeth smoothed an eyebrow. "Cancer." She paused. "Pancreatic."

"I'm sure it had to be devastating for you." Elena could only imagine how difficult it was to watch someone die a slow death from the hideous disease, while being helpless to do anything about it aside from hoping to make them as comfortable as possible.

"It was." Her head slumped. "Still trying to come to terms with it, you know."

"It's a process that will take some time." Elena knew this both from experience and the many stories she had heard before and since becoming a grief counselor.

"Having you to help walk me through the stages of grief, or whatever, would be a big help," Marybeth said thoughtfully.

"I can do that," Elena promised her. "Together, we can deal with this head-on and find solutions that should get you past the worst of it and back on an even track."

Marybeth touched her glasses timidly and managed a tiny smile. "I'd like that."

After finishing up with Marybeth, and then two more clients, Elena thought about taking a walk before her afternoon session. Though the area was usually bustling with locals and tourists alike during the day, given the fact that a serial killer was on the loose and targeting women who resembled her, she thought maybe that wasn't such a good idea. Or was she being overly paranoid, putting a dent in her independent spirit?

When her cell phone rang, Elena looked at it and saw that it was Logan. Her heart did a little leap and dance. She answered. "Hey."

"'Hey' back to you," he said and waited a beat, making her curious if there was more news on last night's victim. Or worse, if someone else had been murdered. "I was wondering if I could make you dinner tonight since our outing last night was cut short."

"I'd love to have dinner with you tonight," she answered enthusiastically. *So he can cook—how nice*, she mused. "But I'd like to bring the wine."

"Feel free to. Pick whatever color you like." Logan's voice sounded amused. "In fact, I'll be heading over to the farmers' market on Kamehameha Avenue to get some fresh items for the meal. If you're free later, say around three, three-thirty, we can get a head start and meet up there and you can help me pick out what works for you."

"Sounds like a plan." Elena actually thought the timing was perfect, as she had no clients scheduled after two o'clock. Plus, it might be fun to pick and choose the ingredients for the meal together. Almost like a real couple, even if they weren't there just yet.

When three o'clock came around, Elena did not see Logan at the agreed-upon spot. She suspected that he may have gotten tied up with work, so she decided to check out the latest at the farmers' market on her own. She looked with interest at some *hamakua* mushrooms, hydroponic lettuce, organic spinach and rambutan—all appetizing. Just when she was about to move on and check out other vendors, Elena spotted out of the corner of her eye a tall figure wearing a hoodie. The person barreled toward her and, before she could react, in an instant she had been shoved hard to the ground at the same time her handbag had been grabbed by the assailant. The last thing Elena remembered just before her head slammed into the concrete was the sound of Logan's powerful voice, though she could not make out the words, and his rushing toward her like she was the most important person in the world, his handsome features an interesting mix of concern and anger.

Chapter Six

The moment Logan saw the tall male, wearing a dark hoodie and dark clothing, moving toward Elena at a brisk pace, he knew she was in trouble. But he was not close enough to them to thwart the danger. Instead, Logan could only warn Elena of the impending threat, even as he raced to get to her. She seemed to respond to the sound of his voice, but barely had time to look in his direction as the assailant body-slammed her. As she went down, the man in the hoodie snatched the handbag she was holding and took off.

Caught between a rock and a hard place, Logan was furious that the brazen daytime robber should target Elena, who was only at the farmers' market at his request. *Damn you*, he cursed within. This made him all the more determined to nab the culprit. But first things first. He needed to make sure Elena was all right. Lifting her up into his arms, he could see that she was shaken up. "Did he hurt you?"

"My pride more than anything," she joked, and

put a hand to her forehead. "I am feeling a little dizzy, but I think I can stand on my own two feet."

Taking her at her word, Logan stood her up. She didn't appear to be wobbly. That was a good thing. "I'm sorry this happened," he said, feeling guilty that he couldn't get to her in time.

"I was just in the wrong place at the wrong time. I'll be fine," she insisted, "provided you can get my handbag that he took. It's expensive and my cell phone and other things I'd rather not have to buy again were in it."

"Say no more." Logan led her over to a bench and demanded that she stay put, even if she felt perfectly okay. Given that she seemed to have hit her head pretty hard, he saw no reason to take any chances before she was checked out. But he needed to make things right, and so he honored her request to retrieve what was taken from her. "Be right back—"

With that, Logan took off in the direction of the thief. At the same time, he got on his cell phone and reported the crime, described the suspect and demanded that the arrest of Elena's assailant be given top priority. *Assuming I can't get to him first,* he thought. Being familiar with this particular farmers' market, which he liked to go to for fresh fruits and vegetables, Logan considered the escape routes a suspect might take. He sensed that this wasn't the perp's first time stealing. Success gave him the confidence to stay the course, as he believed himself to be nearly invincible. More troubling to Logan was the fact that the suspect's clothing and hoodie matched the description of the unsub seen running away from the scene of two of the murders attributed to the Big Island Killer. Could they be one and the same?

With an even greater sense of urgency, Logan took a shortcut, anticipating the suspect's escape route. Bingo! He spied the perp, still clutching the berry-colored designer leather shoulder bag as though his life depended on it, as he moved casually through the crowd inconspicuously. Logan suspected Elena's attacker was only biding his time before bolting to safety to enjoy the fruits of his labor. *Think again*, Logan mused. Without warning, he charged toward the suspect like an angry bull, taking him down hard and giving him a dose of his own bitter medicine. Easily gaining control of the suspect, Logan wrapped his arms around his back and, after handcuffing him, announced with rancor, "You're under arrest." He read the perp his rights and hauled him up without incident at about the same time the cavalry arrived in the form of two uniformed officers.

Forty-five minutes later, Logan was in Elena's hospital room at the medical center, where she was taken for precautionary measures. He was still peeved that the robber had laid a hand on her. The good news to Logan was that he was able to return Elena's handbag to her. As far as he could determine, it still had all its contents, which she had verified. "How are you feeling?" Logan asked again, as if she hadn't heard him before and indicated she would survive.

"Terrific!" Elena flashed her teeth convincingly. "Just a slight headache, but nothing I can't overcome with a good night's sleep."

Logan wondered if that meant their dinner at his place was off tonight. Probably so, he figured, given that he needed to interrogate the suspect as both a thief and possible serial killer. As Logan gazed at Elena on the hospital bed and contemplated whether or not the universe was trying to tell them something, the doctor came in. An African American, Dr. Wellington was in her thirties and slim, with long brunette hair in large and low curls. After checking Elena out, she told her, "You've suffered a mild concussion, Ms. Kekona."

Elena lifted an eyebrow uneasily. "That's good news, right, considering?"

"Yes," she said in earnest. "Especially after you apparently took a nasty blow to the head, according to Detective Ryder."

"Must be that hard head of mine. It worked in my favor this time," Elena quipped.

"Must be." Dr. Wellington smiled. "You won't need to stay in the hospital overnight, but I recommend you take one or two days off from work to rest—the best medicine for this type of injury."

Elena frowned, as if the thought of being away from work was tough to bear. Logan understood where she was coming from, as his work had become his life over the years. He was beginning to wonder if that was a good thing for either of them. Particularly when life could be snatched away so quickly. Smelling the roses, so to speak, had become even more important to him. But only if he had someone special to smell the sweet fragrance with.

"Whatever you say, Doctor," Elena said acquiescently.

"Do you have someone who can drive you home?"

Logan was just about to volunteer for the job, having driven Elena to the hospital in his car, when he heard a strong male voice say over his shoulder. "I will…"

Pivoting to his right, Logan saw a tall and slender man in his late twenties with dark hair in a tight fade cut and a stubble beard walk up to the bed. "Hey, sis, you look like crap."

"Thanks a lot." Elena gave him a disapproving look and turned to Logan. "This is my brother, Tommy." She paused, seemingly ill at ease. "Tommy, this is Police Detective Logan Ryder."

They sized each other up and Logan had the distinct impression that Elena's brother was not too fond of cops. He wondered if there was a story to that. Sticking out his hand, he said in a friendly tone, "Nice to meet you, Tommy."

"Yeah, you, too," he responded with a less-than-enthusiastic inflection, but shook hands, anyway, before turning to Elena. "So, what exactly happened?" She had phoned him en route to the hospital and tried to convince him it wasn't necessary to come. Apparently, he'd thought otherwise.

"I was accosted at the farmers' market by some creep," she explained. "He stole my handbag." She drew a breath and gazed at Logan. "Detective Ryder was able to arrest the thief and return my handbag. Nothing seemed to be missing, thank goodness."

"Mahalo, for helping my sister out," Tommy told him genuinely.

"No problem." Logan wanted to say that his interest in doing so went well beyond an official capacity. But something told him that Elena would rather break the news of the personal nature of their involvement to Tommy in her own way and time. He had to respect that, given that he had no siblings to deal with when it came to matters of the heart. He only hoped that they could get past this awkward moment and continue to move forward in getting to know one another in romantic terms. "Well, I'd better get back to work," he said, wishing otherwise. "I can have someone bring your car home, if you like…"

"I'll take care of that," Tommy volunteered, almost territorially.

Logan nodded. Eyeing Elena, who looked uncomfortable, he said, "When you're feeling up to it, we'll need you to come down to the station to provide a statement regarding the attack."

"I will." She smiled tenderly at him. "Thank you, Logan, for everything."

He nodded again, happy to hear her refer to him

by his first name, suggesting a more personal involvement between them for her brother to contemplate and deal with. That would have to do, for now. Logan left the hospital, already making plans to reschedule their dinner date, if Elena was willing. At the moment, he was eager to grill the suspect, while considering if he could actually be the Big Island Killer as well as a common thief.

ELENA SAT QUIETLY in the passenger seat of Tommy's Volkswagen Atlas, still reeling from her rather harrowing experience with the robber at the farmers' market. She still felt a little sore, but counted her blessings that things hadn't ended up much worse. At least she would live to see another day. The same couldn't be said for the three women who'd died at the hands of a serial killer terrorizing the Big Island. *I could just as easily have been one of them*, she thought, knowing the similarities among the victims. She was glad to know that Logan was out there trying to track down the culprit, sworn to do his duty as a member of law enforcement; even while grateful that he had been there to witness her attack, protect her from further harm and nail the thief before he could rob another unsuspecting person.

Her mind wandered to the date they had planned that evening that went awry, through no fault of either of them. She wondered if Logan was as disappointed as she was that they were unable to have dinner at his place. Did he believe the forces were somehow working against them? Or was it more a case of "if at first you don't succeed, keep trying"? After all, if things were meant to progress between them, wouldn't they still be able to give it a go and see where it went, no matter the hindrances? Could one of those hindrances be her brother? She had seen him tense up when introduced to Logan as a police detective, as though he would be his natural enemy. It was for that reason she hesitated to go further in trying to fix what was likely a nonexistent division between Tommy and him—she hoped to ease into the topic. And there was no time like the present to start.

As if reading her thoughts, Tommy broke his silence. "So what's up between you and the detective?"

"We're friends," Elena said simply, which was true, since they hadn't gone much further than that up to this point, no matter how strong the vibes were between them.

"Since when did you start hanging out with cops?" he asked hotly, peering over the steering wheel.

Not liking the tone of his voice, she responded tartly, "I don't *hang out* with cops. Logan just happens to be in law enforcement. There's a difference."

"Where did you meet, anyway?"

"We met in the course of my work." Elena saw no reason to get into specifics in divulging the confidential nature of their initial meeting without Logan's approval. Besides, there was no reason to justify their friendship to her younger brother, no matter how much she loved him and wanted him to at least like anyone she became involved with, were that to ever happen with Logan in a serious way.

Tommy grunted. "You like him, don't you?"

"Yes, I do." Might as well put it out there and make her brother grow up at the same time. "While we're just getting to know each other, I think I'm old enough to choose my own friends or whatever."

"Never said you weren't," he huffed.

Elena decided she may as well seize the moment. "In fact, if my memory serves me correctly, I seem to recall you telling me recently that it was time I start dating again. Not to say that we're dating," she added quickly, even if they were leaning in that direction.

"Yeah, I know." He paused. "Do what you want. It's your life."

They picked up where they left off once inside her house. Elena ignored some grogginess and told him, "Yes, it's my life. Just as it's your life. I don't tell you who to go out with. So, please, don't try to tell me."

"All right, all right. I get it." Tommy bobbed his head yieldingly.

"Do you?" She fixed him with a hard stare, though believed she had made her point.

"Yeah, I do." He ran a hand across his mouth. "Just be careful," Tommy warned. "I don't want to see you get hurt."

"Logan won't hurt me," Elena insisted. "He's a nice guy. You might actually like him, if you can just get past your prejudices against the police."

"Not sure that's going to be happening anytime

soon." Tommy wrinkled his nose. "Too much history there. Anyway, I'll hitch a ride with a friend and go get your car."

"Thanks." She forced a smile.

"If you get sick or anything, let me know."

"I will," she agreed, "but I'm sure I'll be fine."

Elena saw him out and all she could think of after her experience was wanting to soak her aching bones in a nice hot bath. *I'll also need to go and give a statement to the police about my encounter with the thief,* she told herself. But for now, in following the doctor's orders, she needed to get some rest before rearranging her counseling schedule for the next two days. It would give her plenty of time to read and think about how she could make up for the lost dinner occasion with Logan. Now that she had smoothed things over with Tommy somewhat, as far as the detective was concerned, the time might be right to flip the switch and invite Logan over for dinner. Then the ball would be in his hands as he continued on the offense in search of a serial killer.

"WHAT DO YOU THINK?" Aretha Kennedy asked Logan, as they gazed through the one-way window at the suspect. He had been identified as thirty-six-year-old Gregory Roarke, and had a long criminal record of assaults, robberies and drug-related offenses in Hawaii, California and Nevada. Authorities had been seeking his arrest on a number of charges, including a string of local break-ins and thefts. Though they had him dead to rights on these offenses, Logan was less certain that he was the Big Island Killer. In spite of his penchant for violence related to robberies, Roarke did not have a history that suggested he was prone to being a serial killer. But then, not all serial murderers left a road map that was predictive of future behavior.

"Let's just see what the perp has to say," Logan responded noncommittally, wanting to keep an open mind, even while keen on making sure the suspect felt the full weight of the law for attacking Elena.

"He's definitely not going to be able to worm his way out of this," Ivy Miyamoto said confidently. "At least not for the crimes where the forensic evidence and witnesses point directly to him."

"You've got that right." Logan furrowed his brow and entered the interrogation room with Aretha. Handcuffed, Gregory Roarke sat at a metal table. He was tall and gangly. With the hoodie down, he had slicked-back brown hair, parted in the middle, and gray eyes. He glared at the investigators.

Logan stared back at him with equal rancor as he took a seat next to Aretha across from the suspect, who had been read his rights, including the right to a lawyer whenever he wanted one. "You're in a boatload of trouble, Roarke," Logan said, making himself clear, while seeing how much they could get out of him. "The charges you face are off the charts." The suspect remained mute, as if this would somehow get him out of the jam of his own making. *Not a chance,*

Logan thought resolutely. "Robbing someone at a crowded farmers' market. Not your smartest move, pal. The fact that I witnessed the crime taking place makes it even dumber, as I'll be your worst nightmare when you go on trial for this."

Roarke scowled. "You're scaring me to death," he hissed sarcastically.

"You should be scared," Aretha argued, peering at him unblinkingly. "You're facing hard time and it's not very nice where you're going." She paused. "Being a serial killer is a whole different ballgame..."

The suspect's eyes grew wide. "What?"

"You heard me. We've been looking for someone wearing a hoodie and dark clothes, like the ones you have on, who's been going after young women in Hilo and beating them to death. If you're ready to confess to being the Big Island Killer, it would certainly make our job a whole lot easier."

"Whoa," Roarke spluttered nervously. "I didn't kill anyone. I'm not the Big Island Killer!"

Logan leaned forward. "I'm afraid your word alone isn't good enough in this case. Convince us we're way off base—we need rock-solid alibis and more."

By the time they were finished with the interrogation and some verification, Logan and Aretha had come to the conclusion that Gregory Roarke was a serial offender, but not the serial killer they were after. The suspect was turned over to other detectives in the Area I Criminal Investigations Section who focused on burglaries and home invasions.

Logan sensed they were on the wrong track in attributing the serial murders to Roarke, but it was incumbent upon them to not leave any stone unturned in the pursuit of the unsub. At his desk, Logan gave Chief Watanabe a brief update prior to tomorrow's task-force meeting. "We hoped we had him, but as of now the Big Island Killer remains at large," he explained.

Watanabe jutted his chin. "So, you stick with it until the right perp is taken into custody—hopefully, sooner than later."

"That's the plan." Logan was glad they saw eye-to-eye on staying the course, even if there were detours along the way. He told him about Elena's encounter with Roarke, but left out the fact that they were starting to get involved. At least for now. Logan knew that he was free and clear to date the counselor, should they go in that direction, which he hoped for.

"Good thing you got the perp." The chief's nostrils flared. "And glad to hear that Elena's going to be okay."

"So am I." Logan couldn't hide his relief that she hadn't been hurt badly by Roarke in the process of stealing her handbag.

"By the way, I meant to tell you that Elena sent in her report indicating that you were successful in managing your grief after losing Hideo Zhang, meaning you're able to go about your job with the PD without being distracted in that way."

Logan grinned, happy that Elena had made it official. "Good to know. Elena was a big help in getting me to come to grips with my emotions. I owe her a ton of gratitude."

Watanabe laughed. "Well, that is her paid profession, so I wouldn't have expected any less from the counselor."

"Point taken." Logan left it at that, not wanting to get too carried away. Especially when it was the woman herself that was capturing his fancy even more than the grief therapist.

When he got home, Logan called Elena. "How are you feeling?"

"Better." She sounded good. "Just had a hot bath."

"Great." He conjured up erotic thoughts of them bathing together, before putting them in check. There would be other times, hopefully, to go down that road and back. "Thanks for letting the chief know that I'm no longer mentally unbalanced," Logan joked.

Elena chuckled. "You were never that. Just in need of some rechanneling of your emotions."

"Whatever the case, it worked. I can mourn the loss of my partner and play the role of police detective at the same time." *And can also manage a relationship*, he told himself.

"Exactly," she concurred.

Logan gave her a rundown on where things stood with the man who attacked her. "Since we have other witnesses to the crime, including myself, it won't be necessary for you to come and give a statement after all," he told her, wanting to take the pressure off, as well as give her more time to recover from her ordeal.

"Are you sure?" Elena asked.

"Positive. We've got it covered." Logan took a thoughtful breath. "Sorry this whole thing ruined our dinner date."

"Me, too." Her voice was filled with sincerity.

"I was hoping I could make it up to you." He thought about the cold shoulder he'd received from her brother. Would that impact Elena's willingness to go out with him? Logan wondered.

"I think it's more the other way around," she said, surprising him.

"What did you have in mind?"

"Dinner—Friday night. Only I'd like to cook for you."

The notion lit Logan's face with excitement, even if it was two days away. "I accept your invitation, as long as I get to bring the wine," he said with a chuckle.

"It's a deal," she agreed, chuckling back at him and the nice role reversal from their failed first attempt at having dinner.

Logan got her address and, though he loved talking to her and probably could have done so all night, he didn't want to stand in the way of her beauty sleep and full recuperation. "I'd better let you go," he told her persuasively.

"All right," she said. "See you on Friday at seven."

"I'll be there," he promised.

After hanging up, Logan made dinner for himself, using what he had picked up before going to the farmers' market. The chicken long rice and lomi lomi salmon went down easier knowing that he and Elena would have another shot to do it right. He planned to make the most of it, wherever that led, and refused to allow a killer at large to take away the basic things of life, such as trying to see if there was someone out there Logan could connect with. A person such as Elena.

Chapter Seven

The following morning at the task-force meeting, Logan stood before the large screen display, where he used the remote to show the faces of Liann Nahuina and Daryl Renigado, the first two victims of the Big Island Killer, as a prelude to the third victim, Yancy Otani. He put her image on the screen and immediately couldn't help but see the resemblance to Elena, albeit a few years younger and a different hair color. "Her name is Yancy Otani. Two days ago, the twenty-five-year-old graduate student was accosted at Onekahakaha Beach Park in broad daylight. The murder weapon was a large piece of lava rock used by the perpetrator in an act of blunt-force head trauma to the victim. It's similar to the bludgeoning deaths of Liann Nahuina and Daryl Renigado, though in each instance the murder weapon was different. Nahuina was attacked with a bat and Renigado a wooden mallet. But the MO is close enough that the likelihood is high that we're dealing with a single unsub here—"

Logan put on the screen a still shot of a tall, slender person wearing a dark hoodie and dark clothing, with dirty white tennis shoes. "This person was seen running from the scene of Daryl Renigado's murder. Unfortunately, we can't see the suspect's face, or even hairstyle and color." After taking a breath, Logan said, "A person with a hoodie, clothing and body type matching the description of the person of interest was also seen running from the area where Yancy Otani's body was found." He switched to another image of a tall and slender individual wearing a hoodie and dark clothing and continued, "This was taken by a surveillance camera outside the restaurant where Otani worked part-time and was at, prior to jogging to the park. As you can see, the unsub is hiding in plain sight with the face obscured by shadows and the hoodie. We believe this person of interest followed Otani to the park, beat her to death with a lava rock, and is the same one spotted fleeing the crime scene."

Logan's brow creased, as he felt the frustration of everyone in that room. "Whoever this unsub is, we need to uncover their identity and bring them to justice, with more Hawaiian women vulnerable to being targeted for death." On that note, while the sense of urgency settled in, as if this wasn't already a priority, he called FBI Agent Kennedy to come up.

After she gave a briefing on the Bureau's actions in working with the task force, Aretha introduced a former FBI criminal profiler turned serial-killer crime consultant named Georgina Machado. A Latina and a bestselling author in her early forties, she was on the slender side, and had long black hair in a brushed-out curls style. With three murders and counting attributed to one killer, leaving no ambiguity in defining it as serial in nature, she had been asked to come in to provide a general profile of the Big Island Killer for some added perspective on the unsub to assist in the investigation and apprehension. For his part, Logan wanted to hear what she had to say, having read her book on serial killers with interest. He was open to anything that could add to the investigation in an effort to nab the killer before others had to die needlessly.

"Thanks, Agent Kennedy and Detective Ryder, for inviting me to join the task force pursuing the Big Island Killer," Georgina said coolly. "I've had a little time to study the homicides and behavioral pattern of the unsub in creating a profile of the person we're looking for that I hope will be helpful in the ultimate capture of the killer. First of all, let me say whether it be such monsters as Albert Fish, Henry Lee Lucas, Arthur Shawcross, Jerry Brudos and Robert Hansen, or black widows Belle Gunness and Lydia Trueblood, or even prostitute-turned-serial killer Aileen Wuornos, virtually all are sociopaths who don't need much to get them going.

"In the case of the Big Island Killer, the unsub is fueled by rage over some real or imagined wrong that's been done to them," she asserted, "be it a jilted

lover or otherwise failed romance, irrational obsession, workplace-motivated assault, or a simple act
of revenge on steroids, as one is never enough. This
disturbing behavior caused by the pain and internal
conflicts is being relieved through the malevolent
and largely unprovoked attacks. Given the similarities between the victims, obviously the killer is targeting women of Hawaiian persuasion, whom the
unsub blames for whatever significant event or circumstances triggered the homicidal tendencies…"

Logan listened as members of the task force posed
relevant questions to the criminal profiler, before he
asked one of his own. "So what, if anything, can potential targets of the unsub do to avoid getting caught
in the crosshairs?" If he could do anything to keep
Elena out of harm's way, Logan would certainly pass
it along to her.

Georgina angled her head musingly. "You can't
change who you are, unfortunately," she said candidly, "as it relates to the vulnerable group. That
being said, I'd say the best way to avoid this serial
killer is to not make yourself an easy target, such as
walking around day or night alone, or being isolated
for a killer to strike and leave with no one being the
wiser or little to no resistance. Last, but certainly not
least, one should never be too trusting of strangers or
let their guard down in situations where it should be
just the opposite. Could mean the difference between
life and death at the hands of a serial murderer."

"Should all else fail, being able to legally protect

oneself is a must when confronting a predictable enemy such as this one," Aretha added knowledgably. "The Bureau certainly doesn't encourage violence or use of firearms by or against anyone. Or, for that matter, taking the law into your own hands. But if it comes down to surviving a serial killer or succumbing to one, it's pretty much a no-brainer."

Logan agreed. He also understood that not everyone was mentally or physically equipped to fight fire with fire. Which played to the advantage of killers, such as the one they were hunting. How might Elena fare if confronted by the Big Island Killer? Would she be able to adequately defend herself?

"So why pick on Hawaiian women?" Ivy asked the consultant. "As a Japanese American, I'm not too far removed from my Hawaiian female friends. Are we talking about prejudice for the sake of it, or what?"

"I doubt it," Georgina responded with an air of confidence. "It's not about prejudice, per se. I believe it's personal. The unsub has chosen women who, perhaps by chance, best fit the narrow window at the center of the attacks. It could have been any racial or ethnic group, but does give us a gateway through which we can pinpoint our focus in the investigation."

When the task-force meeting was over, Logan felt they were still on the same team and of the same mind in their pursuit of a relentless killer. Though that was a good thing and Georgina Machado had given them added insight into the unsub's warped mind, this did little to allay Logan's concerns that the worst of this might not be behind them. If the perp's actions were a ticking time bomb, they needed to do everything in their power to keep the unsub from detonating it one victim after another.

AFTER A DAY and a half being cooped up inside her house while recovering from the mild concussion she had suffered at the hands of a robber, Elena welcomed an opportunity to get back out and on with her life. Friday afternoon, she arranged to meet with Leilani Zhang at the Liliuokalani Gardens, a nearly twenty-five-acre, attractively landscaped Japanese oasis in Hilo. It was lush with arched bridges over fish ponds, gazebos, pagodas, rock gardens, and meandering paths over lava flows and tide pools. Throughout the park, there were Japanese stone lanterns and sculptures, and torii gates with amazing views of downtown Hilo, Hilo Bay and Moku Ola, or Coconut Island, a small islet within the bay. Elena saw this as an ideal and safe setting for some nature therapy, as well as an opportunity to get to know a new friend.

"I can't believe you were attacked at the farmers' market." Leilani's mouth hung open with shock as they crossed a bridge.

"I know, right?" Pushing up her sunglasses, Elena could barely hide her own disbelief, knowing the market was normally a hospitable environment. "I guess he thought of me as an easy mark and went for it. Apparently, he had been responsible for a string of similar attacks in the city and elsewhere."

"Just glad you weren't seriously hurt." Leilani tilted her canvas bucket hat, further blocking the sun.

"So am I." Elena considered the person perhaps most responsible for coming to her aid, or at least in taking the perpetrator into custody. "Logan played a big role there. I honestly think the attacker freaked out when he saw him coming his way, fleeing before any more damage could be done."

"Guess it pays to be in the company of a handsome detective who can cook," teased Leilani as they moved past the bridge and enjoyed more of the setting.

Elena blushed, though found it hard to argue the point. She had told her about the dinner date, knowing that Logan and Leilani had gotten closer as friends following the death of her husband, Hideo. "I suppose so," she concurred. "But his cooking for me will have to wait a bit longer as I've invited him to dinner tonight."

"Oh, really?" Leilani fluttered her lashes. "Sounds romantic."

"It's just dinner." At least Elena tried to keep telling herself that. The truth was she was attracted to Logan and felt it was mutual. So why not let it play out and see if there was any fire after the smoke. Especially now that things were out in the open with Tommy and he had begrudgingly chosen not to make waves based on his own experiences with the police.

"Even if you two went beyond a nice meal, there's nothing wrong with that," Leilani told her. "Logan has been on his own for a long time and so have you. There's no harm in seeing how compatible you might be."

Elena laughed. "No harm at all." She hoped someday Leilani would be able to find someone new in her life, and realized it was too soon for the widow to look past losing Hideo. The thought of going it alone for the rest of one's life was not something Elena would wish on anyone. She used the short pause to turn the conversation back toward Leilani as they headed down a winding path, where a gecko put on the speed to cross over ahead of them. "So how are you doing?" Elena asked, as they passed by a stone sculpture.

Leilani sighed. "I have my good and bad days," she confessed. "Talking with you has definitely helped me find ways to be more creative in getting beyond the hurt."

Elena took that as a good sign that the therapy was working. "In my personal experience with loss, I certainly found that using my creative juices constructively was an excellent means to move on."

"And what directions have those creative juices sent you in?" Leilani eyed her curiously.

"I'm reading a lot more these days," Elena said. "Also love to hike, run and swim."

"Not much of a reader, runner, or hiker, but I do

enjoy swimming and scuba diving, though I haven't done much of either lately."

"Maybe you should." Elena took this opening. "We can swim together and you can teach me how to scuba dive."

Leilani beamed. "I'd love to."

"Then it's settled." Elena thought about a neglected pastime she hoped to get back into: kickboxing. She wondered if that was something Logan might be interested in as a hobby. Or was his life way too busy to think and act too much outside the box?

After picking up items for a traditional Hawaiian dinner, Elena went home. She was admittedly a bit nervous about cooking for someone other than Tommy for the first time since Errol's death. But she was more excited about the prospect of having a quiet meal with Logan, hopefully without the drama of duty calling or being a victim of a robbery. *Is that really asking too much?* she mused half-jokingly.

Using cooking and food skills she learned from her mother, Elena prepared kalua pork, poi, squid luau and purple sweet potatoes, with haupia for dessert. She hoped it all met with Logan's approval. Realizing she had run short on red alaea salt to season the food, Elena expected she could get some from Tommy, assuming he was home. She let the meal simmer and stepped out to go to the *ohana*. Spotting his car, Elena breathed a sigh of relief. *Good, he's here*, she thought.

As she approached, the door opened and Tommy

came out with a woman. Both were giggling like children. When her brother saw Elena, his eyes widened and he said, "Hey. What are you doing here?"

Feeling somewhat embarrassed for dropping in unannounced, she responded, "I was hoping I could borrow some alaea salt."

"Of course. Help yourself." He grinned awkwardly and faced the other woman. "This is Kat. She's with the band—"

Elena gazed at the lovely young Hawaiian woman, remembering her from the children's hula dance group at the shopping mall, where they provided the music. She also recalled that the keyboardist had a boyfriend. Her long black hair was in a fishtail braid and her brown eyes sparkled like jewels. "Aloha."

"Aloha." Kat faced Tommy and her eyes popped wide, as though she was eager to leave.

"We're going dancing," he said, reading Elena's mind.

"I see." Elena wondered if Kat had moved on to Tommy as her romantic interest.

"You can come if you want." Tommy eyed her guiltily.

Elena smiled thinly. "Mahalo, but I already have plans for the evening."

He raised his chin contemplatively. "Well, have fun. I know we will."

"I'm sure you will." She wondered just how long this one would last. "I'll go get that alaea salt."

"No problem. Be sure to shut the door on your way out."

"I will." Elena watched briefly as they walked away, before heading inside the *ohana*. Judging by the empty beer cans strewn about, it was evident to her that Tommy and his bandmate had started the party before going dancing. Elena wrinkled her nose in judgment, but pushed back on her assessment. Far be it for her to try to micromanage her younger brother's life, any more than he had the right to dictate whom she decided to spend time with. He was entitled to his choices in companionship, just as she was hers. It was on that last thought, with Logan in mind, that Elena smiled while getting what she came for out of the wooden kitchen cabinet.

She headed back to the main house and continued preparation of the meal, before heading upstairs for a change of clothing. Elena hoped it would be an evening where they could get to know each other better without any interruptions.

Chapter Eight

"You clean up nicely," Elena told him, her cheeks lifted in a sexy smile as she stood in the entryway.

Logan grinned at the compliment, having ditched his detective wear to put on a blue striped dress shirt and khaki pants to go with a pair of brown monk-strap oxfords. He'd even shaved for the occasion, wanting to look presentable on what amounted to their second attempt at a real date. "So do you." He drank in the sight of Elena in a body-flattering fuchsia bandage dress and black mule loafers. Her long and layered dark hair was loose and fell over her shoulders attractively.

"Mahalo." She flushed. "Please come in."

If Logan had been impressed with the outside of the property, with its lush landscaping and fruit trees, he was just as enamored with the house's interior in one sweeping glance. "Nice place."

She smiled, thoughtful. "Sometimes I think it's too big for one person."

"I can relate," he said sincerely. "My house is

the same way, albeit a different style." *I'd love to have someone to share it with*, Logan thought. He stretched his arm out, holding a bottle of Hawaiian guava wine. "This is for you."

Elena took it from him, studying it. "Good choice."

He was glad to hear her say that. "I thought so."

"The food will be served shortly, along with this wine," she said. "Why don't you make yourself at home."

Logan nodded. "I will." He watched her head to the kitchen and was tempted to follow. Instead, he took her up on making himself at home, and walked around a bit, admiring the place. It occurred to him that she must have lived here with her late husband. Instantly, a streak of jealousy shot through Logan at the thought that Elena had been in love with another man. He realized how dumb that sounded, considering he was her husband and Logan hadn't been in the picture to win her over first. But maybe there was a chance that he and Elena could both get a second shot at love.

After the food was laid out, they sat on upholstered cappuccino-brown chairs around a retro wooden table in the dining room. A stationary gecko made itself at home on the wall, barely noticeable to Logan as he dove in to the meal. "Delicious" was all he could think to say in defining the meal in one word.

"Thanks." Elena beamed. "All the credit must go

to my mother, who taught me the finer things on traditional Hawaiian cuisine."

"She taught you well." He smiled and thought that
this was something he could get used to. As long as
Elena came first and foremost with the food. Logan
imagined any such involvement would also need to
include Tommy as her next of kin. "So, what's with
your brother?" Logan hoped this was a good time
to clear the air.

Elena kept her fork with squid luau in the air.
"Excuse me?"

"I could be wrong, but I got the feeling he didn't
like me very much when we met," Logan told her. "Is
it a protecting-big-sister thing…or just me?"

"It's not about you in particular," she said with a
catch in her voice. "And has nothing to do with protecting me from getting hurt."

He regarded her. "Then what?"

She paused thoughtfully. "When Tommy was
younger, he had a run-in or two with police officers.
Since that time, he doesn't really trust the police."

"Sorry to hear that." The last thing Logan needed
was to be looked upon as the enemy by a sibling of
the woman he was attracted to. "He has nothing to
fear from me."

"I know," she said confidently, setting her fork
back on the plate. "Deep down, I think he knows it,
too. We talked about it and Tommy won't be a problem for us. Trust me."

"Good." Logan showed his teeth as he sliced into

the tender kalua pork. Maybe he had gotten carried away with his analysis of her brother. "I do trust you, Elena, and feel comfortable being around you."

"I feel the same way," she gushed, lifting her fork again, this time with a couple of slices of purple sweet potatoes.

Logan felt as though they had cleared a potentially major hurdle in moving forward. He wouldn't kick a gift horse in the mouth, but he was feeling good again at the prospect of having someone in his life. The only obstacle left was a serial killer who didn't seem to want to give the Hawaii PD a moment's peace. And, by extension, the native Hawaiian women of Hilo.

As if reading his thoughts, Elena asked over her goblet of wine, "Anything new with the Big Island Killer investigation...?"

After dabbing a napkin at the corners of his mouth, Logan decided he should be frank with her. "Other than the latest victim, we're at a standstill as far as identifying the unsub," he admitted.

"Sorry to hear that." She frowned. "I've seen the creepy image of what looks like a man wearing a hoodie. Sooner or later, I'm sure someone will come forward who recognizes him."

"I sure hope so." Logan ate more food. "We thought the man who attacked you could be the Big Island Killer. But that didn't pan out." He watched as she appeared to be reliving her ordeal. "The good news is the perp faces multiple charges and, with any luck, will be put away for a long time."

Elena's features eased back to normal. "Good. He deserves everything he gets."

"I couldn't agree more." Logan wanted to avoid the evening being turned upside down by talking about crime and criminals, so he tilted the conversation back to more personal topics. "Tell me what your interests are."

He listened as she talked about being a hiker, runner, swimmer, kickboxer and avid reader. When his turn came, Logan relayed his love for hiking, too, as well as riding horses, snorkeling, working out at the gym and traveling.

Elena jumped on that last passion. "Where have you traveled?"

"When I was working with the California Department of Justice's Human Trafficking and Sexual Predator Apprehension Team, I spent time in Central America and Eastern Europe working with our partners to try and keep a handle on the flow of international trafficking. It gave me an opportunity to see the good side of people living in the countries I visited."

"Sounds fascinating," she said, sipping her wine.

"It was. I hope to visit Australia and New Zealand someday if the opportunity presents itself."

"I'd love to visit those places, too." Elena smiled at him and Logan thought it sounded like she might be open to visiting them together. "And maybe Japan

again, having visited there when I was in college."
She looked across the table. "I hope you saved room
in your stomach for dessert. I made haupia."

"Sounds good." Logan grinned. "Think I can
handle it."

Elena smiled back. "I was hoping you'd say that."
She stood and cleared the plates to make room.

After finishing dessert, they stood with their gob-
lets of wine and moved to the great room. "This was
nice," Logan remarked, grateful that there had been
no interruptions, as they stood close enough to kiss.
He could feel his heart pounding, as desire to be with
her threatened to overwhelm him.

"I agree." Elena raised her chin, as if daring him
to claim her mouth with his. "Kiss me," she demanded before he could react on his own.

"With pleasure." Logan set their wineglasses on
a rustic side table, then cupped her taut chin and
brought their lips together. This time, there was no
stopping him from probing Elena's full mouth deeply
with his tongue, tasting her wine and naturally sweet
juices. Their bodies hugged tightly and Logan felt
Elena's breasts and hard nipples pressed against his
chest, making him all the more eager to take her to
bed. Was she ready for that, as well?

Several minutes of going at it breathily only
heightened his libido, then Elena pulled away. Her
eyes locked on his ravenously. "Do you want to take
this upstairs?"

He held her gaze. "Do you have to ask?" The urgency in his voice, Logan hoped, would tell her everything she needed to hear.

"Who's asking?" She gave him a coquettish look. "Let's go."

Elena took his hand and he followed her as they scaled the curved wood staircase, moved down a hall and into the spacious master bedroom. Logan gave a cursory glance at the antique furnishings before locking in on the king-size platform bed. Elena took away his view by grabbing his face and giving him another passionate kiss. Unlocking their mouths again, she murmured with anticipation, "Do you have protection? If not, I—"

"I have it," Logan told her succinctly. He had been prepared in case such an occasion arose. It had, and he fully embraced what was about to occur between them—taking their relationship to a whole new level. They kissed again lustfully, as the storm of unbridled passions overtook them.

SINCE WHEN HAD she become so assertive sexually? Elena wondered boldly, as she unbuttoned Logan's shirt, exposing his well-developed upper body, as if to tease her for what he brought to the table with the rest of his package. She slid the dress from her own body, exposing herself to him in only underwear and bare skin. His blue eyes darkened with the expectation of seeing her nude. Though she would normally have felt self-conscious at the very thought of being naked for someone other than her late husband, Elena felt just the opposite with Logan. Something about him and his attraction to her made her feel not only comfortable in showing him everything, but it was also a big turn-on that seemed to bring her sexuality to life. This carnal instinct rose a notch or two in her own overwhelming desire to see him from head to toe.

When they were both completely naked and standing before one another, on full and inviting display, Logan said in a throaty voice, "You're absolutely gorgeous."

Elena took in his rock-hard body and handsome face with equal fascination. "So are you," she uttered unblinkingly.

"I want you," he declared bluntly.

She quivered at the prospect, knowing she wanted him just as badly. "You can have me."

As though this declaration unleashed everything they were holding back, without prelude, Logan gripped Elena's shoulders and angled his face to kiss her ardently. Opening her mouth to meet his head-on, she felt the potency all through her body as their lips joined as if belonging together in a perfect fit of delightful sounds of yearning. Grabbing one of her buttocks, Logan brought the two of them even closer together as the kiss intensified. Elena gasped as her hardened nipples brushed stimulatingly against his chest, causing waves of delight to radiate through her. She wasn't sure how much more she could take before she exploded with joyous release. Surely he felt the powerful need as well to be inside her and make love to her.

As if reading her mind, or perhaps sensing her bodily reaction to the mouth-to-mouth intimacy, Logan broke the lip-lock and yanked aside the double-brushed microfiber duvet cover, exposing the sateen-cotton sheet. He then lifted Elena off her feet and gently put her down on the bed. Sliding beside her, Logan said smoothly, "I want to make sure you're pleasured first before losing myself to desire in making love to you."

Before Elena could argue, wanting them to experience the orgasm together, she found herself succumbing to Logan's skillful hands as they caressed her breasts and nipples, making her want to scream with sensual delight. That wave of satisfaction tripled when his fingers moved down between her legs and began to fondle her there with torturous precision. The climax that followed both surprised and thrilled Elena in its intensity and the need to complete it with him inside of her. "Please, don't hold back any longer," she cooed urgently. "Let's do this together—"

"With pleasure." Logan's face was contorted, indicating the difficulty in showing such willpower. He got to his feet and swiftly retrieved the condom from his trousers, placed it upon his erection and came back to bed ready to finish what he started.

Going in for the kiss, Elena seized his lips, exchanging tasty tongues, as Logan sandwiched himself between her splayed legs and lowered his trembling body onto her. They locked eyes lustfully as he drove deep inside and she cried out when he repeated this process of undulating pleasure time and time again, until they climaxed simultaneously. Their ragged breathing slowed down gradually as their heartbeats returned to normal. Only then did they separate and lie side by side, regaining their equilibrium.

Afterward, Logan kissed Elena's damp shoulder. "You were incredible."

She blushed and responded truthfully, "So were you."

"Helps when you're so in sync with another person."

"Now we're in sync, huh?" Elena said teasingly, even while agreeing wholeheartedly. She wasn't sure she had ever been more in sync with someone sexually in her entire life. What did this say about her marriage to Errol? What didn't it say?

"Yeah, I'd say we definitely are." Logan ran a hand along her thigh. "And to think, I nearly balked at the idea of seeing you for counseling." He grinned salaciously. "Glad I didn't let stubbornness get in the way of what might have been the biggest mistake of my life."

Elena laughed, though she was touched by his words. "Not sure that would have qualified as your biggest mistake, but I'm happy too that the chief convinced you to come my way." She giggled. "Of course, I'm sure this wasn't exactly what he had in mind when recommending my services."

"Probably not." Logan chuckled, resting his hand on her knee. "But some things in life require taking your own initiative."

"Oh, you think so, do you?" Elena's eyelids fluttered flirtatiously as she ran her fingers across his chest.

She got a reaction out of him. "Yeah, without a doubt."

"And what might that initiative be telling you now?" she asked, noting that he, like her, was starting to get aroused again.

"That a second go-round might be nice—very nice, at that." Logan's voice sizzled with renewed desire.

"Hmm…" Elena shivered at the prospect of a repeat performance. Only this time, she imagined it would be even more rewarding, now that the elemental urges of the first time had been thoroughly quenched. "I can hardly wait," she murmured, happily giving in to mutual desire and the gratification that promised to come as a result.

To say he wasn't more than ready to make love to Elena again would be unimaginable to Logan, as he fought to contain himself while they kissed, caressed and stimulated one another. He started on top but wound up on the bottom as they went at it hot and heavy, like gladiators doing battle in the arena of sexual attraction. With his hands latched on to her slender hips, Logan guided Elena over him, filling her with the solid heat of his manhood. He let her take charge from that point on as she rode him like the type of dependable stallion he hoped to own one day on his plot of land. He fondled her breasts, perfectly sized as they were, and taut nipples, and heard Elena's breath quicken at the stimulation. His own breathing became erratic as the sex brought her down and their bodies molded into one, moving frenetically while climaxing in lockstep. When it was over, they lay there, her on top of him, for a long moment while catching their breaths, and then slowly returned to the world they had managed to block out like a shade from the sun.

Afterward, still exhausted, Logan held Elena in his arms and they remained silent, as if no words were truly necessary to describe what spoke for itself in their hot and hotter actions. He wanted to ask her where had she been all his life, but knew it was too clichéd. She had been with another man and, for a time, Logan had been with another woman. But that was then and this was now. Whatever the past, he knew that he wanted a future with Elena. Logan believed by her reaction to him that she would be open to this, too. And, hopefully, her brother would give it his blessing. If only for the sake of making Elena happy.

As Logan mused about this, his mind wandered to the Big Island Killer investigation and where it stood. Three women were dead, victims of blunt-force trauma. And one killer was still at large looking for more women to target for the kill. It was something Logan was determined to bring to a halt, if his skills as a homicide detective meant anything. He would return to it full throttle tomorrow. For now, he just wanted to relish the moment with a gorgeous and sexy woman in his arms sound asleep.

Soon Logan joined her in slumberland. Until the sound of his cell phone ringing snapped him into consciousness. Glancing at Elena, whose pretty head rested comfortably on his chest, he noted she was beginning to stir. Wishing they could just remain that way forever, reality told him otherwise and Logan managed to slide from beneath her without Elena waking fully. He took a few steps in the nude to his pants on the floor, where they'd wound up last night, and found his phone. The caller was Ivy Miyamoto.

"Yeah," he answered, while watching as Elena's eyes opened and she gazed at him apprehensively, as if sensing that the call was related to the case he was working on. After listening to Ivy, Logan responded laconically, "Okay. I'll be there as soon as I can—"

"What happened?" Elena's brow creased with worry as she leaned up on one elbow, and her naked upper body caught his eye.

Logan swallowed thickly and said in a flat tone, "A woman, identified as a native Hawaiian, has been reported missing. Apparently, she never made it home last night…"

Chapter Nine

"Her name is Kakalina Kinoshita," Ivy said over the speakerphone as Logan headed to the missing woman's address. He had just come from his own house, where he'd taken a shower and put on a fresh set of clothing. "According to her parents, Daniel and Valerie Kinoshita, whom she lived with, Kakalina was out with a friend, but always checked in through phone calls and text messages to let them know she was okay. When they heard nothing at all from her by morning, they became worried and filed a missing-person report. Could mean nothing," she emphasized. "But given that the missing woman apparently fits the description of the Hawaiian women targeted by the Big Island Killer, it seemed worth checking out—"

"You're right." Though in most instances they preferred that a person was missing for at least twenty-four hours before devoting manpower to investigate what usually turned out to be someone who was not really missing at all, but simply hadn't bothered to inform anyone of their whereabouts, Logan understood the necessity and urgency of investigating right from the get-go, in case the disappearance may have been connected to their serial-killer case. *For her sake, I just hope she's safe and sound somewhere*, he thought. "I should be there in a couple of minutes," he informed Ivy, who was meeting him at the home on Hawaii Belt Road in North Hilo.

"All right," she said and disconnected.

Logan gazed contemplatively through the windshield. Yes, he lived for the hard cases, never backing away from a challenge that required relying on his investigative skills to solve. But the Big Island Killer case was one that was starting to get to him in more ways than usual. It was becoming personal, making it all the more critical that they catch the unsub. Logan thought about Elena, the main source of his added uneasiness in the investigation. The night they had shared had been everything he could have asked for and so much more. She was as wonderful in bed as out of it. The closer they got, the more he couldn't bear the thought of anything happening to her. They had a chance to build something special. He would be damned if he let a serial killer destroy that.

When Logan drove up to the residence, Ivy was already outside, ignoring a light rain that had begun to fall. He got out and walked up to her. "The missing woman didn't happen to show up by chance, did she?"

Ivy shook her head. "Afraid not."

Dear Reader,

I am writing to announce the launch of a huge **FREE BOOKS GIVEAWAY**... and to let you know that YOU are entitled to choose up to FOUR fantastic books that WE pay for.

Try **Harlequin® Romantic Suspense** books featuring heart-racing page-turners with unexpected plot twists and irresistible chemistry that will keep you guessing to the very end.

Try **Harlequin Intrigue® Larger-Print** books featuring action-packed stories that will keep you on the edge of your seat. Solve the crime and deliver justice at all costs.

Or TRY BOTH!

In return, we ask just one favor: Would you please participate in our brief Reader Survey? We'd love to hear from you.

This FREE BOOKS GIVEAWAY means that your introductory shipment is completely free, even the shipping! If you decide to continue, you can look forward to curated monthly shipments of brand-new books from your selected series, always at a discount off the cover price! Plus you can cancel any time. Who could pass up a deal like that?

Sincerely

Pam Powers

Pam Powers
For Harlequin Reader Service

Complete the survey below and return it today to receive up to 4 FREE BOOKS and FREE GIFTS guaranteed!

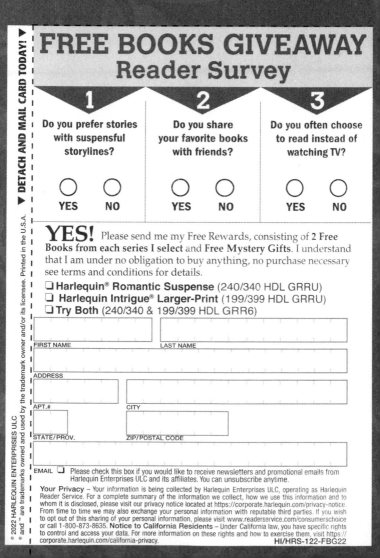

▼ DETACH AND MAIL CARD TODAY! ▼

FREE BOOKS GIVEAWAY
Reader Survey

1

Do you prefer stories with suspensful storylines?

○ YES ○ NO

2

Do you share your favorite books with friends?

○ YES ○ NO

3

Do you often choose to read instead of watching TV?

○ YES ○ NO

YES! Please send me my Free Rewards, consisting of **2 Free Books** from each series I select and **Free Mystery Gifts**. I understand that I am under no obligation to buy anything, no purchase necessary see terms and conditions for details.

❏ Harlequin® Romantic Suspense (240/340 HDL GRRU)
❏ Harlequin Intrigue® Larger-Print (199/399 HDL GRRU)
❏ Try Both (240/340 & 199/399 HDL GRR6)

FIRST NAME

LAST NAME

ADDRESS

APT.#

CITY

STATE/PROV.

ZIP/POSTAL CODE

EMAIL ❏ Please check this box if you would like to receive newsletters and promotional emails from Harlequin Enterprises ULC and its affiliates. You can unsubscribe anytime.

No harm in wishful thinking, Logan told himself. "You never know in these types of cases."

"True." Ivy studied him curiously. "Hope I didn't take you away from anything—or anyone—this morning, Ryder."

Logan imagined that he and Elena might have had another round or two in bed had his overnight stay not been cut short. But being in law enforcement and its, at times, frustrating demands was what he signed up for, so he couldn't complain. At least not openly. "Nothing I couldn't handle or hadn't expected," he responded coolly. "Let's see what the parents have to say."

They walked past swaying palm trees onto the covered lanai of the single-story country-style home on a cul-de-sac. Before the bell could be rung, the door opened. "You the police?" asked a short Hawaiian man in his early fifties with a shaven head and a black chevron mustache.

"Yes, I'm Detective Miyamoto," Ivy said, "and this is Detective Ryder. And you are?"

"Daniel Kinoshita. Please come in."

They stepped into a sunken living area with colonial-style furniture and vinyl plank flooring. A thin Hawaiian woman in her late forties with thick short black hair in a blunt cut entered the room. "This is my wife, Valerie," Daniel said, moving up to her, as if to keep her from falling on shaky knees.

"You reported your daughter, Kakalina Kinoshita, missing?" Logan asked, eyeing the couple.

"Yes, she didn't come home last night," the father pointed out. "That's not like Kakalina."

"We're afraid something bad may have happened to her." Valerie's voice shook.

"That may not be the case at all," Logan assured them, knowing he had little to go on at this point to give them false hope. "How old is your daughter?"

"Twenty-eight," Daniel said matter-of-factly.

Old enough to go off and forget or choose not to inform her parents, Logan considered. "I understand that she went out last night with a friend?"

"Yes." Valerie wrung her hands.

"Male or female?"

"Male," she answered tersely.

"Does this male friend have a name?" Ivy peered at her intently.

She shook her head embarrassingly. "We've never met him."

"But you're sure the person is a male?"

"All of her friends are male," Valerie claimed unapologetically. "She just gets along better with men."

Meaning any one of them was a potential suspect in her disappearance, to Logan's way of thinking. At the top of the list would have to be the man she went partying with, or whatever Kakalina got herself into. "Maybe she chose to spend the night with this friend," he suggested. It sounded reasonable to him, all things considered. *Friends with benefits*, Logan mused, assuming it was all innocent and aboveboard and not something nefarious.

"Kakalina has a boyfriend," Daniel said suddenly, as if this somehow made her immune to infidelity. Or making a mistake. "They love each other. He's just as worried about her as we are. Kakalina would never cheat on him…"

Ivy glanced skeptically at Logan and back. "Even if we give her the benefit of the doubt on that front, it still doesn't mean that your daughter didn't crash at this friend's place and simply forgot to let you know she was okay."

"Kakalina wouldn't do that without letting us know," her mother insisted, her eyes watering. "We've given Kakalina her space, but she's never let us worry about her safety. Especially now, with women being terrorized on the island by a killer…" Valerie's voice broke. "Something has happened to her. You have to find our daughter. She may be hurt…"

Or dead… Logan read between the lines of her frightened tone. He was sympathetic, if not entirely convinced that this was truly a missing-person case. Much less, the work of the Big Island Killer. How many young women going out with a male friend— and who liked hanging out with male friends in general—showed up a day or two later with a hangover, but otherwise not the worse for wear? Still, she was missing, and until located safe and sound, all bets were off. "We'll do the best we can," he promised them. "But we need more information to go on. Such as, where did Kakalina go last night?"

Daniel scratched his chin. "They went to a night-club."

"What nightclub?"

"She never told us." He looked at his wife, as if to back him up.

"We don't know which club," Valerie stated. "She liked dancing at different clubs."

"If you can give us the names of any clubs she's mentioned, that would be helpful," Ivy told them levelly.

They named a few of the places and Ivy made a note of each on her cell phone, before Logan asked, "Does your daughter own a car?"

"No, she likes to walk or ride her bicycle," Daniel replied.

This told Logan that it likely meant the friend drove them to the club and wherever else Kakalina may have ended up. Or she met someone else there and went off with them. Then there was still the boy-friend, who may not appreciate his girlfriend spending time with other guys. They needed to talk to him. "What's the boyfriend's name?" Logan gazed at the father.

"Henry Pascua."

"Do you have a number where we can reach him?"

"Yeah, hold on." Daniel took a cell phone out of his pocket.

Logan took down the number on his own phone and asked, "Do you have a recent photograph of Ka-kalina on your cell that you can send me?"

"Yeah." The father nodded and pulled it up. "Just took this last week."

When the image came onto his cell phone, Logan saw an attractive and slender young woman of Hawaiian descent with long, wavy black hair and hazel eyes. She definitely fit the bill of those in the crosshairs of the Big Island Killer, with respect to their general characteristics; apart from the victims' long hair coming in different colors, whether natural or dyed. Had the unsub gotten to her? Logan turned to the parents and tried to put on an optimistic face. "We'll investigate your daughter's disappearance with the seriousness it deserves. In the meantime, if you hear from her or otherwise learn of Kakalina's whereabouts, be sure to contact us right away."

"We will," Daniel Kinoshita promised and put an arm around his trembling wife's shoulders, pulling her closer.

"Please bring Kakalina home," Valerie cried, as if a mother's instinct feared that this might already be a lost cause.

"We'll do our best," Ivy told her, exchanging glances with Logan, as if weighing whether or not their best would be enough. Outside the house, she asked him, "So what do you think?"

"I think we need to locate Kakalina Kinoshita," he said simply. "She's old enough to know better, but young enough to be taken in by a charming man and potentially a killer."

"My feelings exactly."

"I'll track down the boyfriend," Logan said to her. "Why don't you see if we can pinpoint which club she may have gone to, and who was with her."

Ivy nodded. "Will do."

As they went to their cars, Logan had a sinking feeling about the disappearance, even as he found himself pivoting to Elena as someone whose health and well-being had become a priority to him, if it hadn't been before.

ELENA SHOULD HAVE been caught up in the afterglow of the amazing sex she'd had with Logan last night. He had reawakened her own sexuality and imagination in ways she would not have thought possible as a widow who had, at one point, mistakenly believed that with Errol's death that part of her life might be over for good. That obviously was not true. Logan had seen to this with his tender and magical touch, which had brought her to new heights in the bedroom. But as exciting as this was, and where it could eventually lead them as they navigated the waters of uncertainty in moving forward, Elena's thoughts, as she drank coffee in the kitchen, were on the missing woman that had sent Logan off as a police detective. The moment he received the call, she could tell by the tension in his handsome face that he feared the Big Island Killer had struck again. Had he? Or would they find that the missing woman wasn't actually missing after all?

Elena could only hope for the best, as all Hawaiian women would, given that none of them wanted to die prematurely at the hands of a killer. *In my case, I have too much to live for with Logan now a part of my intimate life*, she thought dreamily, pouring the remaining coffee that had grown cold in the sink and rinsing the cup. She went upstairs, brushed her teeth and put her hair up in a low bun, while imagining Logan running his hands sensually through her loose locks last night and seemingly enjoying every moment. When would there be an encore? And what then? Was he ready for anything steady between them? Was she, when the reality of their separate lives set in? She tried not to get too carried away with the twenty questions, thinking it best to allow nature to run its course, wherever that might be.

Leaving the house, Elena noted that Tommy's car was parked outside the *ohana*. She imagined he and the keyboardist he hung out with yesterday made a late night of it. *Hope you know what you're doing, little brother*, Elena thought, mindful of Kat's supposed boyfriend.

Half an hour later, Elena was in her office for her first session, happy for the distraction from Tommy, Logan and the unsettling thought of a missing woman. Nelson Schultz, her client, was seventy-four and grieving over the death two weeks ago of his wife of fifty years, Gwyneth. The retired cultural anthropologist was wiry, and had short and textured backward-swept white hair. He and his wife had settled on the Big Island a decade ago, moving from Arizona.

"I swore to her that I would just keep on living to the best of my ability once she was gone," Nelson uttered painfully, pushing up his rimless eyeglasses. "But that has proven to be much more difficult now that I truly am on my own for the first time in half a century, putting aside three children, ten grandchildren and three great grandchildren…all of whom I love dearly."

"It was never going to be an easy transition," Elena told him as they sat in her therapeutic office. "Couples who have been fortunate enough to be married as long as you have have earned the right to grieve a bit longer than the rest of us." With her own marriage lasting just seven years, a fraction of the time her client had spent with his late wife, Elena found herself as envious of him as she was sympathetic to him and his loss. What she wouldn't have given to have had five, ten, twenty, or more years with Errol before their marriage ended, way too soon. Along with children to reflect their love and bond. She wondered if a second chance, in the form of a new romance, could be just as gratifying over the course of time and the inner workings that came with a committed and successful relationship and the possibility of a family to go with it. "Your wife was lucky to have you, Mr. Schultz," she told him. "And from the way you've described her, you were certainly most fortunate to have had the pleasure of her companionship for so many years."

"You're right about that." The creases in Nelson's face softened. "Gwyneth was the best wife and mother of our children that I could have asked for. I just wish we'd had more time..." He paused emotionally. "But then, isn't that what we all want—just a little more time?"

"If only that were possible." Elena leaned forward and couldn't help but think about those poor women who had lost their lives to a serial killer. Now there was a possibility that another woman could have met the same awful fate. Like her client's wife, they, too, deserved better. "Unfortunately, it doesn't always work that way." She spoken the sad truth and hoped he got it in the way intended. "What's most important now is that you hold on to the treasured memories you have and try to forge new ones with the help of family and friends." These were words Elena tried to live by in her own experience, no matter how difficult the journey.

LOGAN ENTERED THE Pascua Realty office on Kinoole Street. He was immediately approached in the spacious, carpeted suite by a tall, slender man in his early thirties with dark hair in a windblown bob. The man was dressed in sleek, business-casual clothing. "Hi, I'm Henry Pascua," he said. "You must be Detective Ryder?"

"Yes." Henry extended an angular hand and

Logan shook it warily, having spoken to him briefly over the phone and not gotten a good read on him as the boyfriend of the missing woman.

"Why don't we step into my office?"

Logan followed him through the lobby and to a door that led to a good-sized office with modern furniture and a picture window. Without asking him to sit, Henry said tentatively, "You wanted to talk to me about Kakalina, or Kat, as she prefers, which is short for the non-Hawaiian variant of Katherine…"

"As I explained to you over the phone, Kakalina was reported missing by her parents," Logan said, standing flat-footed. "Do you know anything about that?"

"Wish I did." Henry lifted his chin. "The truth of the matter is Kat and I broke up last week."

Logan regarded him with misgiving. "And why was that?"

"She was into another dude," he said straightfor-wardly. "I don't like competing for a girl's affections, no matter how hot she is. Especially when she made it clear it was over between us."

Logan tried to decide if being dumped by her had made Henry angry enough to do her harm. Or did it merely free him to move on with someone else? "What do you know about the other guy?"

Henry shrugged. "Not much. Only that they met at a club and he got her a part-time gig playing hula music at the mall."

"Which mall would that be?"

"The Prince Kuhio Plaza."

"Do you happen to know his name?" Logan asked, wondering if this was the same person Kakalina had gone out with last night. Or could it have been one of her other male friends?

Henry ran a hand across the top of his head. "No, sorry. She never bothered to tell me."

Logan frowned and became curious. "Did Kakalina—or Kat—ever go missing when you were together?"

"Yeah, you could say that." He snickered. "When we were together, one time we flew over to Kauai and spent the night without telling her folks. They went nuts. Guess she managed to smooth things over with them when we got back."

Logan wondered if Kakalina could have decided to go island hopping again with another man. They would check into that. "According to her parents, Kat's only friends were men."

Henry wrinkled his nose. "Yeah, that seems about right. I knew that going in, but we seemed to hit it off, so I looked past her always wanting to be the center of attention with every guy who looked her way."

"Do you think any of them might have wanted to harm her?" Logan asked, an edge to his tone of voice.

Henry shook his head, maybe a little too quickly for Logan. "I know her folks are worried about her, maybe thinking Kat's fallen into the clutches of this serial killer running around. If you ask me, I think

Kat's just being Kat. When she's ready to surface, she will. I wouldn't worry about it too much if I were you."

Giving him the benefit of a hard gaze, Logan took umbrage at Henry's rather cavalier attitude regarding his ex. "When women like Kakalina are being beaten to death by a serial killer, I take it very seriously. Maybe you should, as well."

"Didn't mean to give you the wrong impression." His shoulders slumped. "I hope she shows up, alive and well."

"So do I." Logan's nostrils flared. "Until such time, I'd advise you to stick around in case we need to talk further."

"I plan to," Henry insisted. "If you have more questions, you know where to find me." He pulled out a business card. "And after this is cleared up with Kat, if you're ever in the market for a house, give me a call."

Logan glanced at the card, knowing he wouldn't have any use for it in the foreseeable future. "I can see myself out," he said succinctly, and walked away still feeling empty-handed as far as a solid lead on the whereabouts of Kakalina Kinoshita. He knew that with every minute she remained unaccounted for, the less the chances that she was still alive.

Chapter Ten

In the afternoon, Elena got a text message from Logan informing her that they were still investigating the apparent disappearance of a Hawaiian woman. In noting that less than twenty-four hours had passed since she'd gone missing, and with no signs of foul play thus far, Logan seemed less than convinced that the woman had been abducted. Or was otherwise absent against her wishes. According to the missing woman's ex-boyfriend, this disappearing act wasn't something new for her, making Logan believe she may have gone somewhere of her own accord.

Elena breathed a sigh of relief. Deciding you wanted to get away without informing anyone may have been selfish, but it certainly wasn't a crime. Whereas, abducting a woman against her will was one. Not to mention if the missing woman had fallen prey to the dreaded Big Island Killer. Still, Elena hoped she resurfaced soon, if only to let her parents know she was okay. *That wasn't asking too much, was it?* Elena thought, having seen her last client for the day. It would also give Logan and the others working the serial-killer investigation one less thing to worry about. She could only imagine the stress they were under in dealing with this case, even if Logan did a good job of masking it. The sooner they could put an end to this nightmare, the sooner things could get back to normal on the Big Island.

As she drove home, Elena pondered what it might mean for her and Logan once they could focus more on them and less on their individual lives. Was this what he wanted? Did she really see a future with the detective after one intense night of intimacy? Or had she somehow lost her perspective and misconstrued sex, mind-blowing as it was, with wanting something much more substantive with a man in her postmarried life? *Guess I'll just have to find out where we go from here and not overthink it*, she told herself, while considering whether or not to invite Logan over tonight for a repeat performance. The thought of making love to the man again made Elena hot and bothered. Or would it be best for him to make the first move after what happened between them last night?

AFTER LOGAN WAS forced to abruptly leave Elena's bed this morning, he'd been more than happy to alleviate, if not squelch altogether, her concerns about the disappearance of Kakalina Kinoshita. The last thing he wanted was to have the Big Island Killer case hanging over them like a dark cloud, which was where all roads seemed to lead whenever a Hawaiian woman went missing. Until proven otherwise. No matter how this ended, Logan did not want it to get in the way of the solid foundation he and Elena seemed to be building. That was the worst thing that could happen. If he hadn't known it before, after last night with Elena, he knew he wanted more between them. Much more. She wanted it, too. He could sense that much. Making it work, given their histories and current lives apart, would be challenging. But since when had he ever run away from difficulty? As far as he was concerned, Elena Kekona was more than worth fighting for. He hoped she felt the same way about him.

That evening, Logan met Ivy at the Southside Pub on Waianuenue Avenue. Kakalina Kinoshita had apparently been seen at the club the night before, accompanied by an unidentified man.

"Yeah, I'm sure she was here," said the forty-something bald owner who sported a grayish circle beard, Marcelo Tahutini, as he studied the photo of the missing woman. "She was dancing up a storm after she'd had a few drinks."

"What about the man she was with?" Logan asked interestedly.

Marcelo scratched his chin. "Hmm, let's see… He was Hawaiian or Latino… Mid-to-late twenties, tall, slim, dark-haired, with some hair on his face…" He sighed. "Just a regular dude."

Ivy looked at him. "Do you have surveillance cameras?"

"Yeah. Have to, these days."

"Mind if we take a look at the video from last night?" she asked.

"Not a problem."

Logan followed them into a cluttered back room, where the owner pulled up the video and got to the approximate time Kakalina was thought to be present. For a while, it looked as if they would come up short, until someone resembling her appeared on the screen. "Stop it there," ordered Logan as he peered at the image and compared it to the picture from his cell phone of the missing lady. "That's her," he decided.

"Sure is," Ivy concurred, and asked Marcelo to continue playing the video.

As they watched, it initially appeared as though Kakalina was alone. Or, at the very least, in the company of everyone at the club, but no one in particular. Then someone walked up to her, putting a long arm territorially around her slender waist, before he faced the camera. "Freeze it!" Logan commanded. Marcelo complied and Logan focused on the person, and recognized him, causing his heart to skip a beat. He could barely believe his eyes. Clear as day—or at least clear enough for Logan to make a confident assessment—the man Kakalina apparently went out with last night was none other than Elena's brother, Tommy.

IT WAS ALL Logan could do to remain mute on the identity of the male seen in the video with Kakalina Kinoshita, given what was on the line. It was a line that Logan knew he was dangerously close to crossing, due to his involvement with Elena. Especially with Ivy staring at the video, determined to identify and locate the man. For his part, Logan was just as keen on talking with Elena's brother, Tommy, who was now the chief suspect in Kakalina's disappearance, short of her showing up alive and well before Logan had a chance to speak with him. But he wanted to do so first, before it became official, as a courtesy to Elena. Surely, she wanted to get to the bottom of this, too. Even if it meant the case may be much closer to home than she could have imagined.

Logan had managed to buy himself a little time by making an excuse to pursue another angle, while hoping, if possible, to smooth things over with Ivy later. He left her to study more surveillance video, including footage outside the club that could lead to identifying Tommy's car and license plate. *Hopefully, he'll be able to shed some light on Kakalina's absence without being guilty of any wrongdoing*, Logan thought, as he headed over to Elena's house. He had texted her to say he was coming, adding that it was official business and leaving it at that. Some things needed to be said face-to-face.

After parking, Logan headed to the main house. But not before having a peek at the *ohana*, where Tommy was staying. Noting that a black Volkswagen Atlas was parked by it, Logan assumed he was home, which may or may not be indicative of a person with something to hide. Could Tommy be keeping company with Kakalina Kinoshita, who could have been hiding out here for her own reasons? Resisting the desire to find out, Logan stuck with the plan to inform Elena first. Before he could ring her bell, she opened the door. "Hey," he said in a controlled tone, ignoring the sexual vibes that were still working overtime in her presence.

"Hey." She favored him with a curious, uneasy gaze. "What's going on? Did you locate the missing woman?"

"Can we talk inside?" Logan didn't want to tip his hand, in case Tommy was somehow able to overhear them and was planning to make a run for it if he knew something bad had happened to the missing Kakalina, and that he was responsible.

Elena moved aside and waited for him to enter. Once she closed the door, she faced him and asked point-blank, "Why the cryptic texting? What aren't you telling me…?"

He sighed and smoothed an eyebrow, as though he needed to. "The missing woman's name is Kakalina Kinoshita," he told her. "Her parents informed us that she went out last night with a male friend. We were able to establish that Kat, the nickname she went by, was last seen at a place called the Southside Pub. The person she was with was seen on surveillance video." Logan paused. "It was your brother, Tommy."

Elena sucked in a deep breath. "So what are you saying?"

"I'm saying that, as someone who may have been the last person to see Kat before she went missing, your brother is a person of interest." At this point, Logan didn't even want to think about the implications of a missing Hawaiian woman in relation to the recent murders of native Hawaiian women attributed to a serial killer.

"Tommy would never have hurt her," Elena insisted, as if reading his mind, her voice dropping an octave out of despair. "There must be some other explanation—"

Logan could see that Elena was visibly shaken by this. But there was something more to her reaction. Did she know something? "What is it?" he asked.

She stared at him for a long moment and her voice shook as she answered. "I saw Tommy with Kat last night."

"Where?"

"At the *ohana*. I went there to borrow something for our meal, just as they were headed out to go dancing…" Elena's gaze fell. "Tommy is in a band with her, playing for a hula show at the mall. I got the feeling they were pretty cozy and probably ended up back at his place afterward."

Logan reacted to this disclosure. He wasn't sure if Elena's knowledge of Kakalina was a helpful sign that Tommy was not guilty of anything other than possibly harboring the missing woman. Or if this compromised Elena as a witness to a possible crime in the making. "I need to talk to Tommy," he told her forthrightly. "It would make things a lot easier all the way around if Kat's there with him. I came here first to give you a heads-up."

Elena bristled. "I'd like to go with you."

Logan wavered. "Not sure that would be a good idea."

"He's my brother, Logan," she pleaded. "If Tommy is in some kind of trouble, I need to be there to help him face up to it."

Against his better judgment, but not wanting to burn his capital with her, Logan agreed. "Just so you understand, I'll be questioning him as a police detective. If I determine a crime of any kind has been committed, I'll have no choice but to arrest your brother."

"I understand," she said coldly. "Let's go to see Tommy."

ADMITTEDLY, ELENA HAD butterflies in her stomach as she walked with Logan in stilted silence through the lava-rock-walled entry yard toward the *ohana*. The idea that the woman who supposedly went missing was actually Kat was bad enough. Much worse to Elena was if something bad had actually happened to her and Tommy was somehow responsible for it. She could only imagine what was going through Logan's head. Any missing woman of Hawaiian ancestry was automatically linked to the so-called Big

Island Killer, and would make the detective likely suspicious that one thing could have led to another and, as such, her brother could be a serial killer. Elena didn't believe that for a moment. Tommy couldn't possibly have done the things said to have been done to those poor women. And Kat was someone she could see that he genuinely liked. It seemed as though they had chemistry. Much like Elena felt she had with Logan. But could that be in peril, as the man she'd made love to less than twenty-four hours ago was now bent on questioning her brother regarding Kat's whereabouts? Elena could only hope there was a simple explanation that Tommy—and perhaps Kakalina—would be able to clear up.

Elena knocked on his door, feeling tense as Logan stood beside her, not as her lover and former client, but as an officer of the law looking for answers from her brother that Tommy may or may not have. When he opened the door, fully dressed, she could read the shock in his face as his eyes darted from her to Logan suspiciously.

"What's going on?" Tommy leveled his gaze at Logan.

"Detective Ryder would like to ask you some questions about Kat," Elena told him, curious herself as to how he would take this.

Tommy hoisted an eyebrow. "What about her?"

"Why don't we go inside," Logan said, making it clear that it wasn't a suggestion.

Tommy didn't argue the point, and allowed them

in. Elena was hoping that Kat would be right there, wondering what all the fuss was about, and would let them know that she was perfectly fine and had chosen not to confide in her parents as to her location. But there was no sight of the missing keyboard player, causing Elena's own blood pressure to rise out of concern.

"Will someone tell me what's going on?" Tommy peered at Elena. "Why does he want to know about Kat?"

Before she could answer, Logan said edgily, "Kakalina Kinoshita's parents have reported her missing. Seems as though Kat was last seen hanging out with you last night at the Southside Pub. Where is she now, Tommy?" His eyebrows knitted as Logan gave him an implacable stare.

"I have no idea," he claimed, ending any such thoughts in Elena's mind that he was hiding her in the bedroom. "After we left the club, Kat and I got into a fight—not physical or anything," Tommy emphasized. "Verbal. I told her that flirting with every Tom, Dick and Harry that looked at her twice wasn't cool. She disagreed."

When he paused, Logan said thickly, "You still haven't told me where she is."

Tommy sucked in a deep breath and ran a hand ruggedly across his mouth. "She asked me to let her out of the car," he asserted. "We both probably had too much to drink at that point, so I did as she asked. Then I left and went home."

Elena pursed her lips. "What were you thinking, Tommy?" she admonished. "Why would you leave Kat out there alone knowing there's some psycho going after Hawaiian women?"

"It was only about two blocks away from her house, okay," he retorted. "How was I supposed to know she wouldn't go home?"

"Did you kill her?" Logan moved up to him, gritting his teeth.

"No, never!" Tommy responded. "She was very much alive when I left her, I swear it." He faced Elena. "Look, I screwed up. I should've driven her home, but I can't go back and change things. I'm sure she found someplace else to chill for the night and, once she's past the hangover, she'll let her parents know she's all right."

"For your sake, you better hope so," Logan warned, and added, as though it didn't go without saying, "I'd advise you not to make any plans to leave the island until this is cleared up, one way or the other."

Tommy gave him a mock salute. "Got it, Sergeant. Now if there's nothing else, I'd like you to get out of my house!"

Logan's jaw tightened. "Whatever you say." He angled his hard gaze at Elena and walked out the door, leaving her behind.

She shot Tommy a disappointed look. "I'll talk to you later."

"I'm not going anywhere," he assured her lowly,

masking what Elena saw as concern for the welfare of Kat.

Elena went after Logan, feeling as if she was caught in the middle. In reality, she knew it went far deeper than that, with stakes that couldn't be higher all the way around. She reached Logan at the gate, calling out to him. He rounded on her, almost seeming like a stranger. "If your brother has done anything to harm Kakalina, I won't be able to run interference in keeping him from facing the consequences."

Elena scowled. "No one's asking you for a get-out-of-jail-free card for my brother, Detective Ryder," she shot back.

"Fair enough," he conceded contritely. "We just need to find Kat, make sure she's unharmed."

Elena couldn't agree more. "Whatever you may think of Tommy, and I know he's far from perfect, he did not hurt Kat. It's not in his DNA." In spite of his faults, Elena felt she knew her brother well enough to know that he would not intentionally harm someone. She recalled a time when Tommy had risked his own life to rescue a female swimmer who'd gone under. He refused to be called a hero, insisting that he only wanted to do what was right. That wasn't the sound of someone capable of committing an act of violence against someone he obviously cared about.

Logan's features softened. "I hope you're right about that."

"I'd like to help in the search for her," Elena offered. "Kat could have fallen and hit her head, or worse—"

"We're not quite at the point of needing to put together a volunteer search team," he said. "And while I appreciate the offer, if it should come to that, it probably wouldn't be a good idea for you to get involved on multiple levels. Tommy is still a suspect in Kakalina's disappearance. That alone would create a conflict of interest, no matter how well-intentioned your offer." Logan met her eyes in earnest. "Apart from that, there's still a serial killer on the loose. I'd never want to see you put in danger, any more than you already are by fitting the characteristics of the unsub's victims."

At least he's differentiating the Big Island Killer from Tommy, Elena told herself, feeling that was a positive thing of sorts. It also illustrated Logan's concern for her, over and beyond his investigating her brother. But was that enough, considering? "You better go continue your search for Kat," she told him stiffly. "The sooner you find her, the sooner Tommy can get out from under a cloud of suspicion. And maybe choose a woman without such a roving eye for others."

"Yeah." Logan paused, seeming to mull things over. "Assuming your brother was being straight with me, we'll focus our official search for Kakalina in the area near her home and see what we come up with."

Elena put a hand on her hip and tried to think positively about the situation. What other choice did she have? "When you learn something…"

"I'll let you know." He scratched his neck. "Look, I'm sorry about all this, Elena," he said sincerely. "I hope you know I'm just doing my job."

"I know," she conceded, holding his steady gaze. "And I'm just looking out for my brother. That's what family does."

Logan nodded. He started to say something, but seemed to think better of it and walked away. Elena watched him briefly, wondering if her mention of family had the unintended effect of diminishing what she thought they had. And just what exactly was that? Was there any chance of building a relationship with Logan as long as he was going after Tommy, and possibly trying to hang Kat's disappearance on him, and more?

Chapter Eleven

I probably could have handled things differently,
Logan thought with regret after leaving Elena's property, given the look of distress on her face, as if she had been betrayed by his appearance. The last thing he wanted was to throw up a roadblock in whatever it was that they had going. It wasn't like he'd planned to make Tommy a suspect in a missing woman's case. As it was, Logan felt he was treading on thin ice in trying to balance an investigation into Kakalina Kinoshita's vanishing act with protecting the woman he had developed feelings for. But as long as he was a police detective, he was duty-bound to take what was handed to him and see where it led. He hoped Elena wouldn't hold that against him. Especially should things take a turn for the worse for her brother. But since she presumably knew him better than anyone and was convinced Tommy's only mistake was bailing on his date, for now Logan intended to go on the assumption that Kakalina Kinoshita was

still alive. They just needed to locate her and reunite her with her family.

Logan hung on that last word—*family*—as if it was something that had managed to elude him in the truest sense of the word for much of his life. Elena clearly had that bond with her brother and Logan envied her for that. Someday, he hoped to be able to have a family of his own where the bonds of love and loyalty would be unbroken. There was still a chance that this could come with Elena. But Logan sensed that the road might be a bumpy one at best, if they were to drive down it at all as a united front. He allowed that thought to linger for a moment or two, before phoning in a directive to begin searching for the missing woman along Hawaii Belt Road.

Half an hour later, a team from the Hawaii PD, including a K-9 unit, had arrived and the search commenced, starting approximately two blocks from the residence where Kakalina Kinoshita lived, and going in both directions. This included stretches of open acres and farmland, where a body could have been dumped. Logan hoped it didn't come to that. In the best-case scenario, Kat would emerge from a neighbor's house no worse for wear, aside from being hungover. Better yet would be to get a call from her parents informing them it was a false alarm and their daughter was fine.

When Ivy showed up, the look on her face told Logan she had latched on to information he knew was inevitable. "Surveillance video in the parking lot of the Southside Pub indicated that Kinoshita left the club with the unsub and got into a black Volkswagen Atlas. We were able to get a look at the license plate. The car is registered to a Tommy Nagano—"

"I expected as much," Logan said matter-of-factly. He paused, weighing what would come next. "I spoke to Nagano less than half an hour ago."

Ivy cocked an eyebrow. "What am I missing here?"

"I recognized him from the surveillance video, but needed to be sure."

"Sure about what?" she asked questionably, a hand on her hip.

Another pause and then Logan continued, "I've been seeing his sister, Elena Kekona."

"The grief counselor?" Ivy's mouth hung open.

"Yeah," he confessed awkwardly, wishing he had come clean earlier. At least she was privy to the required therapy with Elena in order for him to keep his job.

"You're still seeing her professionally?"

"Actually, it's morphed into more of a personal relationship." Logan wondered if that was still the case after leaving Elena with things unsettled between them. "Nagano lives in an *ohana* on her property. Keeping that in mind, I went to talk to them both— see what he was willing to say about Kakalina."

"And…?" Ivy asked anxiously. "Don't hold back."

"Nagano admitted to going out with her last night and leaving the club together," Logan said evenly.

"He claims he and Kakalina got into an argument two blocks from her parents' house, where she asked to be let out of the car. Nagano complied and drove off with her very much alive and unhurt."

Ivy rolled her eyes skeptically. "Do you believe him?"

Logan jutted his chin, while considering Elena's unwavering faith in her brother's innocence. Though it was admirable, experience told Logan that kinfolk were not always the best judge of character, no matter how close they were. "I'd rather reserve judgment until we have more to go on, such as the missing woman materializing."

Just then, they were approached by a grim-faced bald officer, who said sourly, "We found something…"

Logan held his breath as they were led to a nearby vacant lot about three blocks from the home where the missing woman lived. About an acre wide, it wasn't dissimilar to Logan's property. Walking across the grassy, mostly flat land, he heard the police dog barking as if sizing up its next meal. When he saw the fully clothed body lying on its back, and the beautiful face tortured in death and surrounded like a halo by wavy, long dark hair, it didn't take much for Logan to realize his worst fear. He was staring into the face of Kakalina Kinoshita.

"My initial assessment is the victim died as a result of blunt-force trauma to the head area," Dr. Bert

Swanson, the forensic pathologist, said glumly. He flexed the black nitrile glove covering his hand. "Consistent with the deaths of the three other women, ostensibly at the hands of the Big Island Killer."

"Can't say I'm surprised at your preliminary finding." Logan furrowed his brow. All the indicators fit like a perfect embroidery. A corpse laid out like yesterday's leftovers. A lead pipe left behind by the killer, bloodied from going to work on the victim as if her life was worthless. The deceased's personal effects, including her cell phone, strewn about the lot, as though to add substance to the crime scene. And perhaps, most importantly, like the others, Kakalina Kinoshita was a native Hawaiian, a telltale sign that she'd been targeted for that very reason. Even if the specifics for such a cruel ending remained a mystery to Logan. As did the identity of the unsub, though Tommy Nagano had moved to the head of the class as the person in the hot seat with respect to her death.

"It's not much of a head scratcher," the pathologist said succinctly. "Your serial killer has struck again, Detective Ryder. The real question is, can you and your colleagues force the perpetrator out in the open before more damage can be done to other Hawaiian women?"

Could be we already have, Logan told himself reluctantly, but he hoped it was otherwise. If only for Elena's sake. "We won't stop trying," he responded, knowing the words were empty without concrete action to back them up.

He watched as crime-scene photographer Martin Campanella methodically took pictures from every angle of the victim, as well as the surrounding area, as potential evidence of the crime—all of which could be used against the unsub once they had him in custody.

"Did I miss anything?" Campanella asked, pointing his lens away from the crime scene.

"Probably not," Logan told him. "But get a few more pics, anyway, including on the road and to the right and left for anything the unsub may have left behind."

"I'm on it."

Logan watched him work for a moment and then turned to the sound of Aretha Kennedy muttering to herself. Then, she said more clearly, "Judging by the location of the body in relation to the victim's home address, I'd say that either Nagano lied about where he says he dropped off Kinoshita, or someone else—the serial murderer—picked her up afterward and drove the victim to this spot before beating her to death with the lead pipe. Different murder weapon. Same MO."

"Maybe someone she knew?" Logan said, hazarding a guess, as he wanted to give Elena's brother the benefit of the doubt for the time being. He couldn't envision even an inebriated Kakalina willingly entering the car of a stranger. Unless it was one whom she viewed as nonthreatening. Given that the immediate area was unlikely to reveal much through home-surveillance videos, their best bet was that a camera might have picked up Kakalina getting out of Tommy's car. Short of that, his story could fall flat.

"Or someone who forced her into the vehicle at gunpoint," Ivy said, tossing out another possibility. "These things happen. Especially if the perp had followed them from the club and seized on the opportunity."

Aretha frowned. "Could be a hard sell, Detective. Particularly when we have a clear suspect in the onetime missing woman's death who admitted getting into an argument with the victim that could have easily gotten out of control." She glanced at the deceased, who was now being carted away under the authority of Bert Swanson. "You heard the forensic pathologist. We're looking at the work of the Big Island Killer. Do the math. Two plus two women bludgeoned fatally equals four and counting..."

It was something Logan could not turn his back on, even if he wanted to. The facts spoke for themselves. He would be interested to see if the victim's cell phone yielded any clues, now that it was being analyzed forensically by the CSI unit. But at the moment, the spotlight was squarely on Tommy Nagano as Kakalina Kinoshita's killer.

"A BODY WAS found in a vacant field," Logan informed Elena in a video chat on her laptop, legs folded beneath as she sat on the vintage cherry accent chair in her great room. He hesitated just long enough for her to read what was coming next. "It's been tentatively identified as Kakalina Kinoshita…" He paused again. "She was murdered in a manner similar to the victims of the Big Island Killer…"

Elena put a hand to her mouth as the implications became loud and clear, and there was a pounding in her ears. "Oh, no, you don't think Tommy killed her…and the other women?" She knew this was exactly what was registering in Logan's strained facial expression. He was insinuating that her younger brother had progressed from some minor skirmishes with the law to suddenly becoming a violent serial-killer psychopath in Hilo. "He didn't do it," she insisted, knowing that her brother would never have so coldly taken another's life, much less several lives, as though undeserving of being among the living. No matter the bleak picture that was painted on a dark canvas.

"So you say." Logan gazed at her coldly. "Whether I believe you or not is immaterial at this point. Given the fact that he was apparently the last person to see the latest victim alive—and now she's dead, not far from where he claimed he dropped her off—we're going to have to bring Tommy in for a more formal interrogation regarding Kakalina's murder, as well as the other murders attributed to the Big Island Killer."

"When?" Elena asked with trepidation.

Logan sighed. "Detectives are on their way to pick him up even as we speak," he warned straightforwardly. "I need you to keep him there until they arrive. The worst thing for Tommy would be if we had to issue a BOLO for his apprehension."

Elena was appalled that he was asking her to be involved in the arrest, in effect, of her own flesh and blood…for murder. *How can Logan expect me to turn him in?* she asked herself. The answer came just as swiftly. As a dedicated detective for the Hawaii PD doing his job, how could he not expect her to do the right thing even if it seemed so wrong? If Tommy was truly innocent, wouldn't they be able to figure it out? If he wasn't, would she be doing him any favors in helping him become a fugitive from justice at the expense of future victims of a serial killer?

"Fine," Elena stated acquiescently. "I'll do my best to make sure Tommy doesn't try to make a run for it." As she realized that suggested he was guilty of something other than letting Kat get out of the car prematurely, she added firmly, "Not that he would, as someone innocent of committing any murders—"

"Good," Logan said simply, seeming to focus more on the first part of her response than the last. He tilted his head caringly. "Will you be okay?"

"I guess that all depends, doesn't it?" She held his gaze. "I just want my brother to be given a fair shake."

"He will be," Logan promised and waited a beat. "I'll let you go talk to him."

Wanting to say more, but unsure what she could do to alter the course of events at this stage, Elena merely nodded before ending the chat. She closed the laptop and sucked in a deep breath, knowing the hard part came now—preparing her brother for becoming the primary suspect in the death of his girlfriend and bandmate. And, even worse, being questioned about any knowledge or involvement in the homicides perpetrated by the Big Island Killer.

SHE PHONED TOMMY and asked him to come over, wishing they could just make this go away. But that wasn't an option. At least not until the authorities questioned her brother and were satisfied that they were reaching for something that wasn't there. Surely, Logan and the police department weren't under so much pressure with the Big Island Killer case that they would seek a shortcut to ending it, even if it meant railroading an innocent man?

The moment Tommy stepped into the house looking bedraggled, as though he hadn't been able to rest all night and day, Elena figured he knew something serious was up. "What is it?" he asked, peering at her.

She sucked in a deep breath and cut to the chase. "They found Kat—"

For an instant, Tommy looked relieved. This was replaced by a sense of dread. "Is she…?"

"She's dead, Tommy," Elena said, finishing for him sorrowfully. "Someone murdered her."

He put his hands to his face and muttered an expletive. "Where did they find her?"

"In a vacant lot a few blocks from her parents'

house." Elena's lower lip quivered. "She was beaten to death in a way that's similar to the murders of the other Hawaiian women blamed on a serial killer."

Fear registered across Tommy's face. "Do they think I killed Kat?" His voice broke. "The others?" He gazed at her. "They do, don't they?"

"It doesn't matter what they think." She was trying to be supportive, even if believing otherwise. "We both know you're innocent. They will, too, after you talk to them."

His brow furrowed as he pondered things. "So the cops—and your boyfriend—are coming to arrest me?"

"Logan's not my boyfriend," Elena countered, but knew that the nature of their involvement was ambiguous. Neither had truly defined it, though she realized they had something between them that went beyond sex. But even that was imperiled by the current situation. Her thoughts turned back to the question posed. It deserved a candid response. "I'm afraid they're on their way."

Tommy began pacing. "The cops are going to try to pin those murders on me."

"Just tell the truth about last night, Tommy," she pleaded. "They can't charge you with anything if the evidence isn't there."

"You don't know that," he responded, agitated. "They do that all the time, put people away to make themselves feel better—guilty or not."

"That's not true. Not in this instance." Elena had

heard about the occasional person being set free after faulty evidence, shady witnesses, or DNA exonerated them. But most who were convicted were guilty as charged. She was convinced that it was the truth that would get the authorities to back off her brother. But not before they would probably put him through the wringer. Until such time, she would stand by him, as any loyal sister should. Elena heard the car drive up, indicating that the police had arrived. The idea of seeing her brother possibly being hauled off in handcuffs made her stomach turn. Worse, though, was having this cloud hanging over him while the real killer of Kakalina, very likely the Big Island Killer, was still on the prowl.

Chapter Twelve

Logan regarded the suspect through the one-way window as Detective Miyamoto and Agent Kennedy interrogated Tommy Nagano. Against his better judgment, Logan had stepped aside in leading the interrogation of the suspect, given his own conflict of interest and needing to do this by the book, whatever the result. He only wished Elena's brother hadn't been dragged into the Big Island Killer probe by way of his involvement with murder victim Kakalina Kinoshita. This, quite naturally, put Logan at odds with Elena, whom he had developed feelings for that had nothing to do with the investigation. Something told him she didn't exactly see it that way. He was left to wonder if they could get past this when all was said and done.

"You did the right thing in letting Miyamoto and Agent Kennedy run with this one," Chief Watanabe remarked beside him. "Hard to imagine that Elena's brother is wrapped up in this murder investigation.

Worse yet is the notion that we could be looking at our Big Island Killer in Tommy Nagano."

Logan flinched. "Elena doesn't believe for one second that he's guilty of anything, other than being at the wrong place with the wrong person at the worst possible time."

"I would expect her to defend her brother to the death," Watanabe said sensitively. "All people tend to believe the best of their blood relatives while dismissing the worst, as though their lives depended on it."

Logan didn't disagree. "The search warrant on Nagano's *ohana* and vehicle came up with nothing to connect him to the Big Island Killer homicides, such as a hoodie or other potential evidence. Or to indicate the premeditated murder of Kinoshita."

"So maybe he got smart and dumped anything and everything that could tie him to the crimes."

"Doesn't seem likely." Logan begged to differ, since he was familiar with the unsub's MO. "If Nagano is our serial killer, he wouldn't have necessarily thought we were on to him to get rid of the evidence. Moreover, using forensic tools for mobile devices, we were able to unlock the victim's cell phone and found no unusual communication between her and Nagano to indicate they had a toxic relationship, or otherwise gave him a reason to want Kinoshita dead."

"Hmm…" Watanabe scratched his pate musingly as both listened in on the interrogation of the suspect, who had yet to ask for legal representation after being advised of his rights.

"Do you really expect us to buy that you just left Kinoshita by the side of the road and went on your merry way?" Aretha asked, peering at the suspect.

Tommy didn't waver. "That's what happened. I wish I could go back and change things, but I can't."

"You mean change beating her to death?" the FBI agent said tartly.

"No way!" he insisted. "I would never have done that to her."

"And yet she was found dead just a few short blocks from where you claimed you let her out of your car." Ivy planted her hands on the table separating them. "How do you explain that?"

"I can't." Tommy put his hands to his head. "Obviously someone else came along and...killed Kat—"

"Doesn't that sound just a little too convenient?" Aretha furrowed her brow. "After all, you've already admitted to being jealous that she was flirting with other men. Is that why you killed her—you just couldn't take it anymore? If you couldn't have her, then no one would?"

"That's crazy!" Tommy's chin sagged. "I didn't kill her. Why don't you find out who did? Or don't you care about getting to the truth?"

Ivy took a breath and changed course in the questioning. "We all want the truth to come out, Nagano. Especially with four Hawaiian women dead, all the victims of blunt-force trauma. We believe they were murdered by the same assailant. Given your direct connection to the latest victim, Kakalina Kinoshita, why should we believe this was just happenstance and you're not the Big Island Killer?"

Tommy's eyes dropped before he said in a defeated tone of voice, "Maybe this is where I ask for an attorney—"

Logan cringed at the thought of a much more drawn-out investigation should a lawyer get involved. The last thing they wanted was to let a serial killer loose. But just as bad would be devoting time and resources to harassing an innocent man. Logan turned to former FBI profiler Georgina Machado, who had come in to assess the suspect. "What do you think?" he asked her.

Georgina wrinkled her nose. "I'm not feeling it with Nagano being our serial killer," she said bluntly. "His story about dropping off an inebriated Kinoshita short of her residence strikes me as a bit weird, but I don't see him as a sociopath. The Big Island Killer has no sympathy for their victims. Just the opposite. This person feeds off their suffering and eventual deaths. Nagano, on the other hand, clearly shows remorse in his actions and the aftermath that resulted in the death of Kakalina Kinoshita." Georgina ran a hand through her hair. "I think we may be looking in the wrong direction here..."

"You may be right." Logan was inclined to agree. But they needed more than gut instincts and profiling before letting Elena's brother off the hook. "Why don't I see if Nagano will agree to take a lie-detector test?"

"If he's really innocent," she said, "that would be a better way to show it than lawyering up."

Taking that cue, Logan stepped into the interrogation room. Ivy and Aretha looked at him curiously. Tommy glowered, his lips pursed in anger. Logan wasn't sure if this was for being there against his will. Or a misguided belief that by virtue, he was somehow betraying his sister. Logan got right to the point. "Would you be willing to take a polygraph test, Nagano, before you call your lawyer? It could go a long way in getting us on the same page in establishing your innocence."

An hour later, Pauline Alvarado, a licensed polygraph examiner for the State of Hawaii, arrived to administer the lie-detector test. In her early forties and slender, with dark hair in a wedge cut with bangs, she told Logan coolly, "Let's just see if Mr. Nagano is being truthful or not..."

"Do your thing," he said to her in earnest, and watched along with Aretha, Ivy and Georgina through the one-way window as the polygraph examiner entered the room where Tommy was sitting alone. She explained the procedure, and got him set up.

After she went through the basic questions, such as name, age and occupation, Pauline got to the nitty-gritty when she asked the suspect, "Did you murder Kakalina Kinoshita?"

"No," Tommy said succinctly.

"Do you know who murdered Ms. Kinoshita?"

"No."

"Did you kill Liann Nahuina?" Pauline asked evenly.

"No, I didn't," he said flatly. She didn't like his response and repeated the question, and got a simple no for an answer.

"Did you kill Daryl Renigado?"

Tommy kept his cool. "No."

Pauline waited a beat, then asked pointedly, "Did you murder Yancy Otani?"

"No," he answered solidly.

The polygraph examiner drew a breath and looked him in the eye squarely. "Are you the Big Island Killer?"

Without hesitation, Tommy declared in no uncertain terms, "No!"

Pauline asked a few more questions, analyzed them and left the room. Logan and the others on the team eagerly awaited her findings. "Let's have it," he said professionally.

Before she could utter a word, Logan had already sensed her conclusion on the suspect in Kakalina Kinoshita's death. "He passed with flying colors," the polygraph examiner asserted. "Unless Mr. Nagano has figured out a way to beat the system, he is neither the killer of Ms. Kinoshita nor the one you are calling the Big Island Killer."

"I suspected as much," Georgina said. "The unsub is much too clever to go down so easily."

"I suppose," Aretha conceded. "Still, we needed to push Nagano to rule him out as the unsub."

"Now that we have," Ivy said, "it means the perp is more dangerous than ever in the ability to track a target, kill with the slimmest margin for error and get away."

Logan's forehead creased. "It also suggests a sense of desperation, which, with any luck, will lead to the unsub's downfall," he said confidently, as the victims of this crazed killer flashed through Logan's mind. But at the moment, he knew they could at least take Tommy off the list as a serial-killer suspect. "I'll drive Nagano home."

THEY RODE BACK in silence for the first few minutes. Then Logan decided he better say something. Whatever it took to try to smooth things over between them. After all, he fully expected they would be involved in each other's lives to one degree or another, if Logan had anything to do with it, considering his desire to be a big part of Elena's life moving forward. In spite of the hit their relationship had taken recently, through no fault of his own. Or hers, for that matter. "Your sister never stopped believing in you," he told him supportively.

"I know that." Tommy was riding in the front seat, which Logan had offered as a courtesy, having been empty for the most part since the death of his partner. "Too bad I had to be hauled down to the police station like some common criminal. Or worse, a murderer."

"It was never anything personal," Logan insisted, keeping his eyes on the road.

"Was to me."

He's going to make this difficult, Logan thought. "Look, Tommy, we're dealing with the cold-blooded murder of someone I presume you really cared about and played music with. I would think that you, of all people, want to see Kakalina's killer caught."

"Yeah, of course."

"In order to do that, we needed to believe your story about dropping her off on the road, so as to concentrate our efforts on the true killer. Do you get that?"

"I suppose." Tommy's tone became more conciliatory. "I never wanted that to happen to Kat." He paused. "Or to those other women killed by this Big Island Killer."

"We're singing from the same hymn there," Logan said, seizing the moment. "But it did happen to Kakalina and the others," he stressed. "Getting to the bottom of it is a priority for the police department. Sometimes that can mean having to put an innocent person through the wringer to eliminate them from suspicion."

Tommy sighed. "Yeah, I get it."

While he believed that, Logan also felt that Elena's brother still had a chip on his shoulder regarding the police, whether warranted or not. "I know you've had your issues with law enforcement in the past, Tommy, but just so you know I'm not your enemy."

He nodded. "Okay."

Good first step, Logan thought. He waited a moment or two and got right to the heart of the matter. "I care about your sister."

"I gathered that," Tommy said sardonically. "She seems to care about you, too."

"Elena deserves to be happy," Logan added.

"Yeah, she does." Tommy left it at that. Logan believed they had turned a corner. At the very least, they could be cordial to one another moving forward, if not friends, as Logan worked toward regaining any ground he had lost with Elena.

IT HAD BEEN hours since Tommy had been taken into custody and Elena hadn't heard a peep from Logan or anyone else in the police department. Not that the man she had slept with, leaving her longing for more, had any obligation to keep her informed on the fate of her brother as a murder suspect. *Or maybe Logan did owe me that courtesy*, Elena told herself, pacing around her great room like someone who was far too unsettled to be still. If they had anything solid on Tommy as a murderer, didn't she have a right to know? Even if he was presumed guilty, her brother was entitled to legal representation. Elena tried to figure out how she might be able to help him pay for a good lawyer. Though she had managed to do well for herself through savings and investments, along with a large sum from Errol's life-insurance policy, lawyers didn't come cheap. But she would do whatever she needed to be there for Tommy, as she knew he would if their situations were reversed. That notwithstanding, Elena clung to the belief that her brother was incapable of inflicting the type of violence on innocent women as had been done by the Big Island Killer.

Her thoughts were interrupted when she heard a car drive up. A peek through the window and Elena recognized it as Logan's official vehicle. Her heart skipped a beat as she wondered if he was there to throw more negative news her way. Or could he actually have something positive to tell her? Only after focusing did Elena realize someone else was in the car with him. A man. It was Tommy.

She watched as both men got out and approached her house, illuminated by the driveway lighting and tiki lights that lined the pathway leading to the door. Tommy did not have on handcuffs or appear as though he was coming to say goodbye as a courtesy from Logan. Racing to meet them, Elena opened the door. Both men stood there with stoic looks on their faces.

"I'm no longer a suspect," Tommy told her measuredly. He looked weary but surprisingly energetic.

As if to double down on that, Logan said in an official manner, "Tommy is free to go about his life."

Elena was practically speechless. In that instant, she wanted to hug both men. Instead, she hugged one—her brother. "I'm so glad to hear that." She pulled away and met Logan's steady gaze, needing more information.

Tommy said perceptively, "I'll let Detective Ryder fill you in on the details. Right now, I could use a hot shower. Maybe a bath, too." He chuckled tonelessly. "I'm going to the *ohana*. We'll talk later, sis." He made eye contact with Logan, shook his hand and said plaintively, "When you find Kat's killer, I want to be there to see justice served."

Logan nodded in agreement and Elena watched as her brother headed off toward the open gate to his place. "Mind if I come in?" Logan asked hesitantly.

She gave him space to do so and he walked by her, then Elena closed the door to face the man who had been her lover and suspected her brother in his girlfriend's disappearance and murder. Now it appeared as if Logan was responsible for getting Tommy released from custody, for which she was grateful. Elena gave him a quizzical look. "So what happened?" Her voice was more inquisitive than demanding.

"Tommy passed a lie-detector test," Logan told her simply. "Apart from that, the search of his premises and car came up with zilch." He met her eyes sorrowfully. "Things just didn't add up in terms of your brother being guilty of anything beyond poor judgment. We had to let him go."

"Mahalo for that," she said, unable to help herself, while resisting a repeat of the I-told-you-Tommy-was-innocent statement that Elena had felt in her heart and soul. She was thankful the authorities came to realize that before it was too late for her brother. "I'm glad Tommy was cleared of any wrongdoing."

Logan moved closer. "I hope you realize that I was only doing my job in investigating Tommy. As the last person, apart from the killer, to see Kakalina alive, I would have been derelict in my duties as an officer of the law if we overlooked him as a suspect. At the very least, we needed to clear him so we could better focus on other potential unsubs."

"I know. I get it." Elena found it difficult to argue with his logic. In her heart of hearts, she understood that in order for Tommy to be removed from the equation, he had to walk through the fire to get to the other side. "You did what you had to."

His features relaxed. "So we're good then?"

She took a moment before responding positively, knowing she didn't want to lose him. "Yes, we're good."

Logan grinned. "Great! That's all I needed to hear."

Elena smiled back thinly. As much as she was thrilled to continue their journey, she still felt as though they were being weighed down by his serial-killer investigation. It had almost pulled her brother under. Would the case prove to be more than their relationship could handle? She asked, "With Tommy no longer considered a person of interest, where are you now in the search for Kat's killer?"

Logan scratched an ear pensively. "Well, for one, given the manner in which she was murdered, we're going under the assumption that her death was caused by the Big Island Killer. That alone gives us more insight into the unsub and the risky moves being made by this person to fulfill this sick need to brutally murder Hawaiian women. Kakalina Kinoshita was unfortunate enough to fall into this deadly trap, with your brother being caught in the undertow."

Elena cringed at the thought of what the women had to endure. "Will this nightmare gripping Hilo ever end?" She was sure he was asking himself the same question.

"Yes, it will end." Logan's voice was forceful. "No killer, no matter how cunning and cruel, can keep it going indefinitely. This one is no exception. When the unsub slips up in the slightest, we'll nail them and bring this case to a close."

Eyeing Logan and the determination in his hardened features, Elena couldn't help but believe him. And stand by him, even with the recent strain that had been put on their relationship. Though she wanted to ask him to stay the night more than anything, it seemed like the wrong way to go, maybe for both of them. "I think I'm going to go to bed," she told him unenthusiastically. "It's been a long day and even longer night."

"I understand," Logan said dolefully, making no attempt to use his charm to talk her into anything he wanted. "I won't keep you any longer."

Before he could turn to leave, Elena cupped his cheeks and did what she had been unable to resist—she planted a firm kiss on his lips. Drawing their bodies even closer, Logan was just as caught up in the moment in giving as much as he received, which made her go weak in the knees. Using all the strength she could muster, Elena managed to detach herself from him and uttered breathily, "Good night, Logan."

He lifted her chin satisfyingly. "'Night, Elena."

She watched him leave, touching her swollen lips, and Elena again found herself fighting to keep from going after him. But in the end, she trusted herself enough to believe that what they had was real and worth waiting for.

Chapter Thirteen

The following morning, Elena took a short hike with Tommy to Peepee Falls, an 80-foot waterfall fed by the Wailuku River and surrounded by lush vegetation and lava rocks. She considered this as nature therapy for her brother, who was in the midst of the stages of grief, even if unaware. Losing someone he was close to in such a violent manner was something he would need to deal with and she wanted to be there to help him get through it.

"It's tough," Tommy groaned, kicking at some rocks. "Robin is torn up about it, too." Robin Oyama was the other male member of their band and played the hula drum. "Kat didn't deserve to go that way."

"No, she didn't." Elena did not pull any punches in emphasizing the nature of the tragic death. Tackling what had happened head-on was the best way to accept and come to terms with the grief her brother was experiencing. "But then, neither did the other victims of the serial killer." Logan had made it pretty clear that the task force investigating the crimes believed that it was all but certain that Kakalina Kinoshita's death was carried out by the Big Island Killer. "Kat and the other women had their whole lives ahead of them before they were snuffed out by a maniac."

"I blame myself for what happened to Kat," Tommy lamented ruefully. "I should never have let her get out of that car."

"As I recall, you only did what she asked," Elena pointed out. "You had no way of knowing that she would meet up with a serial killer that close to her house. Neither did she. We can't control some things that are simply beyond our control." She knew it was more complicated than that. Drinking had played a role in their decision-making on that fateful night. And in that respect, both parties had to bear the blame. Sadly, only one of them had lived to talk about it, and with deep regret.

"How does one get past something this terrible?" Tommy asked. "Or can you really ever get past it?"

"Yes, you can." Elena watched as he kicked more small rocks. "It's never easy and it certainly won't be in this case. But you're young and strong, and can weather the storm of such a loss."

He looked at her. "You mean like you did when Errol died?"

"Yes. His death was not a violent one, but no less painful as someone I loved and never imagined I'd lose so soon."

Tommy put a hand in his pocket musingly. "How are things with you and Detective Ryder?"

Elena raised an eyebrow, not expecting him to ask. "We're trying to get back on track after—"

He cut her off. "If you like him, don't mess things up on my behalf. We talked things through and I believe he's a good guy. Maybe even the right man for you."

"You think so, do you?" She could barely believe her ears. How had Logan managed to convince her sometimes stubborn little brother to cut him some slack as a detective and a man? It certainly made things simpler as Elena thought of possibly building a future with Logan.

"I'm just saying…" Tommy gave a little chuckle.

"Duly noted." She smiled warmly, while hoping that after some time had gone by, he would be able to get past this and his penchant for playing the field, and find someone he could fall in love with and have a family of his own. Elena turned the topic back to dealing with his grief. "You need to go see Kat's parents."

Tommy frowned. "Not sure I can do that."

"You have to," she persisted. "They need closure, too. The only way her parents can get that is if you help them by showing sympathy and letting them know how much you cared for her."

He mulled this over. "All right, I'll talk to them."

"Good." She put a hand on his broad shoulder. "You'll feel better afterward. And if I can be of service to them as a counselor, I'll be happy to help."

"Mahalo, sis." He gazed at the waterfall, as did Elena, as she pondered her next get-together with Logan.

ON MONDAY MORNING, with Tommy Nagano no longer considered a suspect in the murder of Kakalina Kinoshita, the task force was doubling their efforts to home in on others who might be lurking in the shadows as the Big Island Killer and going unnoticed. To that end, Logan and Ivy were pouring over more surveillance video from the Southside Pub, where Kat spent her last night before leaving with Tommy. "See anything?" Logan asked, scanning the image that showed people coming and going, including Tommy and Kakalina.

"Nothing or no one that jumps out at me," confessed Ivy. "Maybe if we take it back further..."

"Wait," Logan said when he spotted what looked like someone in a dark hoodie moving away from the camera. "There—" He pointed at the screen.

"I see the person." Ivy asked Marcelo Tahutini, the club owner, to zoom in on the hooded one. He did and all they could see was the back of someone who was tall and slim. Then the person faded from view. "Rewind," she ordered, hoping to find a different angle.

When that failed, Logan had the owner switch to the outside camera and timed it for when Kakalina and Tommy first left. For maybe thirty seconds there was no indication of anyone else leaving the club.

Then someone moved out swiftly, head bent down in what Logan thought was a clear attempt at concealment. It looked to be the same person wearing a hoodie inside the club. Frustratingly, the unsub moved out of view.

After Tommy's car drove off, it wasn't long before another vehicle sped away in their direction. The video was rewound and frozen to reveal what looked to be a late model black Buick Envision SUV. The driver could not be seen, but Logan believed it could be the possible killer of Kakalina Kinoshita and a string of other Hawaiian women.

They were able to get a read on the license plate and found that the vehicle belonged to Julian Gaskell, who lived at a residence on Haili Street. With time of the essence and a search warrant in hand, police personnel, including the Hawaii PD SWAT team, and FBI agents converged upon the address, hoping to catch a serial killer before he struck again. Logan and Ivy, armed with their Glock pistols, and Aretha, carrying a SIG Sauer P226 sidearm, led the way. They moved past mature sugi pine trees and the SUV parked in the driveway, and approached the front door of the mission-style house.

It opened almost on cue, as if the occupant sensed trouble, and Logan found himself face-to-face with a dark-skinned male about his height and in his midthirties. He had short black hair with a balding crown and a hipster beard. "Whoa…" The man raised his hands immediately, as shock registered across an oblong face. "I think you've got the wrong house."

Logan still had his gun pointed at the man, not convinced his claim was accurate. "Are you Julian Gaskell?"

"Yeah." He flashed Logan a questioning look. "What's this all about?"

"Step outside the house," Logan ordered, hoping the suspect didn't make a wrong move. "Keep your hands up where we can see them."

"All right," he agreed, keeping his arms up while stepping onto the lanai. "Don't shoot!"

Once the suspect was frisked by Ivy and determined to be unarmed, Logan lowered and put away his own weapon and said tonelessly, "I'm Detective Ryder, Hawaii PD." He didn't bother identifying anyone else, but was sure the suspect got the point that they were all law enforcement. "Is there anyone else inside?"

"No, I live alone," Gaskell indicated. "Is someone going to tell me what it is I'm supposed to have done?"

Logan ignored him for the moment while giving the team the nod to check the residence for other occupants or evidence suggesting a serial murderer lived there. While they were at work and the SWAT unit was ready and waiting, he shifted his attention back to the suspect. "Is that your vehicle?" Logan eyed the Buick Envision.

"Yeah," he responded nervously.

"Anyone else been driving it lately?" Aretha asked, taking a crack at him.

"Just me," Gaskell insisted. "Why do you ask?"

"Were you at the Southside Pub last Friday night?" she asked him directly.

"Yeah," he admitted quickly. "Did I break any laws in going out to have a good time?"

"That remains to be seen," Logan told him with reservations. He allowed the suspect to lower one hand in presenting the search warrant that covered the house and vehicle. "Your car was seen following another vehicle from the club. One of the occupants of that vehicle, Kakalina Kinoshita, was later found beaten to death in a vacant lot. Do you know anything about that?"

Gaskell's jaw dropped. "Not a thing!" His voice rose an octave. "I had nothing to do with any murder. I saw such brutality when I was deployed as a member of the US military in Iraq and then Afghanistan. I would never do anything like that as a civilian. I have no idea who this Kakalina Kinoshita is. If I followed the car she was in from the club, it was by chance and nothing more."

Logan couldn't knock his service to the country, if he was telling the truth on that score. Turned out, Logan's own father was a US Air Force veteran. Sometimes soldiers came back messed up and took it out on innocent people. Did that happen here, in the form of a serial killer?

"Where did you go after you left the Southside Pub?" Ivy asked the suspect sharply.

"To my girlfriend's place," Gaskell responded swiftly and surely. "Spent the entire night there."

"Her name?"

"Lorraine Fuentes. She has a condo on West Lanikaula Street."

"We'll check it out," Logan promised. He then got the word that there was no one else inside the house and a search of the Buick Envision turned up nothing suspicious. After the suspect's alibi held up and with no other reason to believe he'd played any role in the death of Kakalina, it became clear to Logan that this was a false alarm. Julian Gaskell was not the Big Island Killer.

"I was wondering if I can take another shot at making you dinner tonight?" Logan asked Elena in a cellphone video chat that afternoon. "Figured after the drama that happened involving Tommy, you could use a break. Or at least a home-cooked meal where you aren't the one doing the cooking."

"Just dinner?" She gave him a teasing look, while sitting in her office.

"Well, now that you mention it, I thought that maybe afterward we could take a hike. There's a great trail right outside my property, and since that's something we both enjoy, it might be a good way to unwind."

Given the tenseness she'd felt lately, Elena didn't

have to think about it twice before answering enthusiastically. "Yes, I'd love to have dinner with you and go hiking." Both would give her an opportunity to get to know him better in his own environment.

"Great." He gave her a polite grin and quipped, "This time, if it's all the same to you, I think it's best we avoid meeting at the farmers' market beforehand."

Elena laughed, even if the thought of being robbed and hitting her head on the ground was anything but funny. She appreciated his dry humor anyhow. "That works for me."

"Somehow, I thought it would." He laughed generously.

"This time, I'll bring the wine," she said jovially.

"Wouldn't have it any other way." The smile on his face faded like the vog that polluted the air on the Big Island, courtesy of the emissions coming from the Kīlauea volcano, which was nothing new for residents. "Well, I'd best get back to it so I don't screw things up this time. See you later."

"You will," Elena promised, and disconnected from the chat. She was tempted to ask him for the latest on the investigation into the death of Kat, which was connected to the Big Island Killer case. Especially now that Tommy had been part of the probe, though since removed from any involvement of a criminal nature. But she'd decided to hold off on that for now, not wanting to put a damper on what she hoped would be an evening to remember more for their spending time together rather than talking about a serial killer in Hilo.

When she arrived at Logan's gated house, Elena was suitably impressed, if not a tad nervous, to be taking the next step in their relationship in his neck of the woods, no pun intended, as the property bordered the Waiākea Forest Reserve. Still, she embraced the opportunity, wanting nothing more than to get past the strain between them after Tommy's detainment. Logan greeted her at the doorway, looking dapper in a casual way in a form-fitting golf shirt and chino pants.

"Hey." He offered her one of his charming smiles and gave her a once-over, causing Elena to blush. With the hike in mind for later, she had put on a tank top and cropped jeans to go with her sneakers, while putting her hair in a loose ponytail.

"Hey." She smiled at him as her heart fluttered under the weight of his nearness.

"Welcome." He moved to the side. "Come on in."

Elena stepped through the door and handed him the bottle of pineapple wine she brought. "Hope this will do."

"Yes," Logan assured her. "Excellent choice. I'll set this in the kitchen and give you a quick tour of the place before we eat."

"You're on." She followed him around and marveled at the interior. The architectural style and Hawaiian furnishings definitely agreed with her, and Elena could actually imagine living here, even with her current house and the memories made there with Errol. But maybe new and lasting memories were meant to be created with a new person in her life.

As if to play on that theme, Logan stopped the tour when they reached one spacious room and said coolly, "This is the master suite."

"So it is." Elena hummed interestedly, as she took in the bedroom with tropical furniture and a wrought-iron four-poster California king bed.

"You like?" He brushed up against her shoulder and Elena felt a tremor throughout her body.

"Yes," she confessed, a fresh surge of desire threatening to overtake her.

"Hoped you would." Logan gave her a teasing look and said, "Why don't we step onto the upstairs lanai so you can take a peek at the landscape."

"I'd like that." Frankly, Elena welcomed the distraction from the man himself. On the lanai, she admired the property's lush acreage and wondered if he planned to do anything with it. Or did that depend on whether there was someone steady in his life to help with the decision-making? "It's amazing," she told him.

"Yeah," he agreed thoughtfully and faced her with earnest eyes. "You're amazing."

She flushed. "You really think so?"

His response was to kiss her and Elena welcomed it wholeheartedly, before Logan broke the spell. "Better get back downstairs. Wouldn't want the food to get cold."

Elena licked her lips, wanting him now. "You sure about that?"

"Not really." He stepped back into the room. "I think the food can wait."

"Yes, it can," she uttered, not being able to take off her clothes fast enough, and neither could he.

They made love with the same sense of urgency as before, throwing themselves into it carnally and with a kind of familiarity with each other's bodies that left Elena breathless and contented. Logan left little doubt that the same was true for him. Dinner came afterward. While eating *kalbi* ribs, ahi poke salad and grilled pineapple, and washing it down with wine, they kept the conversation mostly light. Neither seemed too interested in talking about the Big Island Killer investigation, as if avoiding it would somehow make it go away. At least temporarily.

They ended up back in bed for more of each other's intimate company, and when they finished the satisfying sexual bonding, Elena asked in a giggly voice, "Whatever happened to the hike you promised?"

Logan laughed. "Something more important came up."

"Agreed." She chuckled. "Much more important."

"But if you're willing to spend the night," he began, "we can take that hike in the Waiākea Forest Reserve first thing in the morning."

As she had nowhere better to be and no one she wanted to spend the time with more, Elena accepted his invitation to stay the night, knowing that neither of them was likely to get much sleep or complain about it.

Chapter Fourteen

They were up bright and early to hit the trail. Walking through the misty forest, with its breathtaking views of Mauna Kea, Logan welcomed Elena's company. Last night had been incredible and only made it clearer to him that he wanted her in his life on a much more regular basis. They had gotten over the hump in his business with Tommy, and now Logan wanted only to get past the Big Island Killer case and concentrate on developing a relationship with someone for the first time since Gemma. He had high hopes that this could happen with Elena, who seemed every bit as receptive to building upon the advances they had made.

"I could get used to this," she remarked as they headed down the trail, no one else in sight.

Was there a double meaning there? Logan asked himself. "So can I," he said, leaning more toward waking up with her each and every day, with an active lifestyle together a bonus. "Gives us something to shoot for."

Elena smiled. "Always a straight shooter, I'm sure," she teased him as they made their way down the path surrounded by rich vegetation and exotic trees.

He smiled back. "I try to be."

"Then I'm with you." The sparkle in her tone told Logan she meant what she said, which put even more pep into his own steps in taking this journey toward the future with her.

When Elena suddenly gasped, Logan first thought she might have spotted injured wildlife. Or another hiker in distress. Then he followed the angle of her eyes and homed in on an area off the trail. Sprawled atop foliage was the fully clothed body of a dark-haired female. Judging by the condition of the remains, she had been there for some time. He noted what looked to be a rusty sledgehammer nearby. Acting on his protective instincts, Logan held Elena close to him, sparing her from seeing what he feared might be the work of the Big Island Killer.

"MY GUESS IS she's been dead for a week or more," Bert Swanson, the forensic pathologist, said in his preliminary assessment of the deceased at what had been labeled a crime scene. "The injuries to her head and face are eerily similar to those inflicted upon the other victims of our serial killer."

Logan cringed at the thought. Based on identification found near the body, she was tentatively identified as thirty-two-year-old Paula Hekekia. He had already ascertained from the moment he'd seen her that she was a victim of foul play. Now it appeared this was from blunt-force trauma, the MO of the Big Island Killer, with the murder weapon being the sledgehammer that had been bagged as evidence by Forensics and would be analyzed for fingerprints and DNA. The fact that Elena discovered the body was equally disturbing to Logan—he hated she had to come face-to-face with this kind of death. Not wanting her to be involved any more than necessary in the investigation, he'd called in the crime and then taken Elena back to his house to await his return. She was shaken, but doing her best to remain strong under adverse circumstances.

Aretha peered at the corpse and, frowning, said petulantly, "This is certainly the Big Island Killer's work. Somehow, the unsub managed to strike and keep the murder from being discovered until now."

"Not sure that was the game plan," Logan offered. "More likely, it wasn't the perp's intention to go this long without the discovery of the remains. Somehow it just worked out that way."

"And could have prompted another kill," the FBI agent speculated on the murder of Kakalina Kinoshita.

That thought occurred to Logan, as well. If true, it had set in motion not only Kakalina's death, but also the inadvertent involvement of Tommy in the case. "Does it appear as though the victim was killed where the body was found?" Logan queried, given its proximity to the often-used hiking trail in the forest reserve. "Or could it have been put here by someone?" If so, this would have required some doing and put the unsub at greater risk for detection.

Swanson examined the corpse with his gloved hands, turning her over and back. "In the absence of any visible indications that she was dragged or perhaps tossed into transportation to bring her here, some distance from the entry to the park, I'd have to say that the victim was likely struck at or around her present location. I'll know more after the autopsy."

"I'll touch base with you then." Logan didn't want to wait that long for some answers as to how Paula Hekekia ended up being murdered. And who may have wanted her dead, assuming the crime was planned before the fatal attack was carried out. There had been no other reports of a missing woman recently that would have drawn the PD's attention. And possibly saved the life of the victim. Logan needed to get to the bottom of this if they were to have any hope at all in solidly linking the homicide to the unsub.

TAKE A DEEP breath to calm your nerves, Elena ordered herself, as she sipped on a cup of oolong tea at the soapstone breakfast bar in Logan's kitchen. Just as they had started to bond with nature on a personal level, the last thing she expected was to come upon a dead body in the Waiākea Forest Reserve. Especially one that had all the earmarks of being someone who died violently. With the victim's features distorted with time since her death, and perhaps being further victimized by animals and insects, it was hard to know if she was a native Hawaiian like the others murdered by a serial killer. Or if her death was an entirely separate incident. Either way, it pained Elena to think that the woman, who had long dark brown hair with caramel highlights, she imagined—based on her style of clothing—was probably around her age, with a long life ahead of her, had been murdered. Ending any chance for a worthwhile future life. *All I can do is hope that Logan and the police department find out who killed the poor woman*, Elena told herself, *and bring some type of peace to her loved ones*.

When the front door opened, Elena flinched, as if the killer had zeroed in on her as Logan's lover and houseguest, and was planning to add to his victim count. She relaxed upon seeing that it was Logan himself entering the kitchen. "Hey," he said in a gentle tone, moving right up to her. "Are you all right?"

"I'm alive," she answered sardonically, considering the fate of the woman they located. Elena knew, though, he was only concerned for her welfare. "That will have to suffice for the time being."

He held her sturdily in his strong arms. "I'll go along with that."

"Why was she even there in the woods in the first place?" Elena asked, recalling that her clothing did not appear as if she was dressed for hiking.

"Could have been any number of reasons," Logan

answered. "Just taking a leisurely stroll or maybe she liked the environment."

"Do you think she went to the forest reserve willingly with the person who killed her?"

"That's a possibility. And it's just as possible she went there alone and was accosted and killed by a stranger."

Either way, it unnerved Elena. "Someone must have been looking for her."

"You'd think so. But that might not have been the case." He released his grip on Elena and said thickly, "We'll get the person who killed her."

Elena raised her chin, reading his thoughts. "You think it was the Big Island Killer, don't you?"

Logan paused. "It's a good possibility."

She recoiled while picturing the ghastly remains. "I was thinking the same thing," she admitted, sure it came as no surprise to him, considering the serial killer on the loose on the island.

He didn't try to sugarcoat it. "The MO is the same and the time frame corresponds with the other deaths. We'll know more soon. In the meantime, if you'd like to stay here, chill out for a while, you're more than welcome to."

While under other circumstances Elena might have jumped at the chance to spend more time at his house—in his bed, keeping it warm and ready for him to join her—now she preferred to be under her own roof as this homicide investigation unfolded. "Thanks, but I should go," she told him gently.

"Okay." Logan ran a hand along her cheek and gazed at her keenly. "Just be careful. As long as this case is still active, don't take any unnecessary chances in what you do."

"I won't," she promised, knowing that he had given her a whole new reason to live. She would not let that be threatened by her own actions. "I would ask the same of you. Now that we have something to build upon, your health and well-being is just as important as mine."

"Fair enough." He flashed a sidelong grin and kissed her softly. "I'll be careful out there. I have you to remind me of what I have to lose."

Smiling, she lifted up on her toes and gave him another kiss, ignoring the ominous feeling of danger that suddenly came over her like a shroud threatening what they had.

"THE DECEASED'S LAST known address was a house on Laukona Street," Ivy said as she and Logan walked toward his desk at the station. "According to her landlady, a few weeks ago Paula Hekekia simply dropped out of sight. Apparently, she was unemployed and struggling to pay the bills. The landlady believes Hekekia became homeless."

"Which could explain how she ended up in the woods," he suggested. "Or maybe she just wandered there from the streets and was latched on to by the unsub, who tracked her like an animal, found the right moment to go on the attack and then bludgeoned her to death before making an escape."

Ivy's brow furrowed. "The victim was there long enough to have attracted attention, if the pathologist's preliminary estimates are correct. So why did it take you and Elena to discover the body?"

"I'm still trying to figure that out," Logan admitted. "The most likely thing I can think of is that she was simply missed by hikers, with just enough distance from the main path and shrubbery to block the remains from view."

"Probably not exactly what the unsub had in mind. The killer seems to feed on making a statement, if you will, with the display of the victims of blunt-force trauma."

Logan couldn't disagree. He feared that this would only propel the unsub to act again. And it wouldn't stop as long as there were more women who had the desired characteristics, with seemingly no one able to prevent the murders from occurring. This was something Logan was determined to change, with the alternative being more than he wanted to imagine.

Ivy stopped as they reached the desk. She took out her cell phone. "Paula Hekekia's landlady showed me a photo of the victim that she left behind. Fits right in with the other Hawaiians the unsub has gone after."

When Ivy pulled it up, Logan stared at it. The victim had a long, thin two-toned hairstyle with wispy bangs. Her features—big olive-brown eyes and a dainty nose with a full mouth—were remarkably similar to Elena's, perhaps more so than the other murder victims, causing him to wince. What if she had been the one who crossed the killer's path in the woods? The very thought of Elena meeting her end in such a terrible way was almost more than Logan could even imagine.

Ivy cocked an eyebrow. "What's up? You look like you've just seen a ghost…"

"It has nothing to do with the supernatural." He scratched his chin reflectively. "Let's just say I'm more determined than ever to put an end to the Big Island Killer's murder campaign." Logan left it at that, while steeling himself for the battle ahead to protect Elena from a potential date with death.

"Sorry you had to see that," Tommy said as he consoled his sister.

"No more than I am," Elena told him honestly, having dropped by the *ohana* after a shower and change of clothing.

"I'm just glad Detective Ryder was there to get you through it."

Me, too, she thought. She was becoming more and more comfortable with Logan's strong presence in her life. The fact that Tommy seemed to find it acceptable as well made the promise of tomorrow all the more exciting. But today was a different matter altogether. Hawaiian women were still dropping dead like flies and the authorities seemed no closer to catching the culprit than after the first woman was killed. Or perhaps she wasn't being fair to those tasked with solving the case. Surely, they were pursuing angles toward that end that Elena was not privy to. Could she expect Logan to let her in on every single detail of the investigation? Even if she did have a vested interest, in more ways than one, as a Hawaiian female who was also romantically involved with the detective. "We were both able to come to terms with the reality of the moment," she pointed out. "It was frightening, to say the least. But there was nothing I could do to keep from finding the body."

"If you hadn't, who knows when someone else might have come along and been observant enough to do the same?" Tommy put a hand on her shoulder. "Just don't stress out about it."

"I'll try to heed your advice." Elena kept her voice level. She didn't want to crack, knowing that he was still dealing with the death of Kakalina and needed her to remain strong.

"So does Logan believe the woman was murdered by the Big Island Killer?" her brother asked, curious.

"He thinks it's a real possibility," she told him candidly.

Tommy sucked in an uneven breath. "Is this nightmare going to go on forever?"

"I keep asking myself the same question." Elena paused, then, in realistic terms, said, "I guess it will end when the killer runs out of steam. Or the police gain the upper hand in putting the killer out of commission." She wasn't placing bets either way, but bracing herself for whatever came next.

The following day, Elena attended the funeral of Kakalina Kinoshita with Tommy. In spite of the drizzle, many people showed up to pay their respects, including their bandmate, Robin Oyama. Elena felt for Kat's parents, grieving for a loss that never should have happened, but had, anyway. She offered them her services as a grief counselor, letting them know she was Tommy's sister. He had owned up to his part in inadvertently opening the door to a killer. They had forgiven him and welcomed him to be there in memory of Kakalina and in the spirit of all Hawaiians, who came together during times of need.

Gazing at the mourners, Elena couldn't help but wonder if Kat's killer could actually be among them. Didn't they say that some serial killers got a perverse thrill out of being present when burying their victims, as if pulling one over on law enforcement by hiding in plain sight? Would the person be so bold as to be there? She scanned the faces, trying to identify the culprit. Realizing it was a hopeless effort, Elena tried to relax and refocus on the service, and get through the rest of the day. It wouldn't be easy, as long as the Big Island Killer remained at large, putting other lives in danger.

Chapter Fifteen

"We got what appears to be a hit!" forensic analyst Shirley Takaki exclaimed, as she stood before the large screen display in the conference room the following morning.

Logan's eyes lit up at the news as he looked at her, with Ivy, Aretha and other members of the task force on hand. "Go on..."

Shirley used the remote to click at the screen, showing a sledgehammer. "We were able to collect DNA, apart from the victim's, from the handle of the hammer found at the crime scene where you discovered Paula Hekekia's body, Detective Ryder. The forensic unknown profile came up with a match in the state database with arrestee and convicted offender profiles. It belongs to a Mark Teale, who was arrested a year ago for trespassing, but the charge was dropped."

She put his mug shot on the screen and Logan saw a white male in his early thirties with blue-gray eyes and long, scraggly dirty blond hair, parted in

the middle. Was this their serial killer? The pathologist had confirmed that Hekekia was murdered, had
died from blunt-force trauma to the back of the head.
Her injuries matched with the sledgehammer as the
murder weapon.

Shirley continued evenly, "We put Teale's DNA
profile in the Combined DNA Index System to see
if anything came up and struck pay dirt! The forensic DNA record corresponded with a DNA record
of the suspect in the database. Teale had an earlier
run-in with the law in California for drug possession." She drew a breath. "As to the DNA found on
the sledgehammer, at this point, we don't know if it
could have somehow ended up there before the hammer was used as a deadly weapon. Or if the DNA
belonged to the assailant—"

"I'm betting on the latter," Logan asserted, even
if the suspect's arrests were for nonviolent offenses.
He wanted to hear much more about this Mark Teale.
"A DNA match and an identification is music to my
ears…"

When Shirley seemed to hedge and eyed Ivy sur-
reptitiously, Logan got an uneasy feeling in the pit
of his stomach. He watched as Ivy took over from
there. She uttered bleakly, "Before any of us get too
excited about the suspect being the Big Island Killer,
there's just one small problem…"

"Don't keep us in suspense, Miyamoto." Logan
raised his voice intentionally. "What is it?"

Ivy blinked. "Six months ago, Mark Teale died by

suicide at the age of thirty-four." She put an image of a newspaper article on the screen with the headline, Disgruntled Man Dies at Hawaii Volcanoes National Park from Self-inflicted Gunshot. "Apparently, Teale was depressed and decided to check out by putting a stolen .357 Magnum semiautomatic pistol in his mouth and pulling the trigger," Ivy said, frowning. "So unless Teale was able to come back from the dead as something akin to a homicidal vampire, he couldn't have killed Paula Hekekia in spite of the DNA found on the murder weapon."

"I don't believe in the supernatural," Logan muttered humorlessly, his disappointment evident. "Especially where it concerns murder." He was not quite ready to dismiss the dead man in relation to the crime that had occurred in Logan's backyard, in effect. "What else do we know about Teale?"

"Not much, at this point," Ivy admitted, "though the name sounds familiar. From what I've been able to gather, he meandered between being homeless and working odd jobs on the island, before taking his life."

Logan zeroed in on the crime-scene DNA profile. In his mind, it had to be more than coincidence that it happened to belong to a dead man. "Could Teale have a twin brother?" he asked.

"It's possible." Ivy scratched her head. "Why? You think the DNA could belong to someone else?"

"Someone who may have the same DNA," Logan said speculatively. He directed his attention to Shirley and asked, "Isn't it true that identical twins have the same DNA?"

The forensic scientist responded with authority. "Yes, essentially. A standard DNA test on monozygotic or identical twins will come back with a 99.99 percent similarity, leaving little room for differences."

Logan's eyes widened. "Meaning that if Teale does have a twin brother, there's a good chance the DNA left on the sledgehammer used to kill Paula Hekekia belonged to him and not Mark Teale."

"Yes," she conceded, "that would certainly help clear up the mystery of the DNA and a dead suspect."

"And give us a viable living one," Logan said fervently, "who just may well be camouflaged in clear view as the Big Island Killer."

ELENA WAS ADMITTEDLY curious when Logan phoned to say that there was an interesting development in the case regarding the dead body they found. Without giving anything away, he asked her to meet him at Audra's Coffee House on Kinoole Street. He was already seated when she arrived, but stood before Elena got to the table, giving her a light kiss on the cheek.

"I took the liberty of ordering us green coffee," Logan said, having learned that it was one of her preferred healthy drinks.

She smiled. "Thanks, that was thoughtful of you."

"My pleasure." He waited for her to sit before taking his seat across from her. "I wanted to keep you in the loop with the latest news in the investigation into the death of the woman we found at the Waiākea Forest Reserve…"

Elena picked up her mug with the steaming coffee. She wondered if they had a lead on the killer. If so, were they certain that the perpetrator and the Big Island Killer were one and the same? "What's happening?" she asked eagerly.

"She's been identified as Paula Hekekia, age thirty-two. According to the autopsy report, she's been dead for about ten days, a victim of foul play." Logan tasted the coffee, waiting for it to go down. "Apparently, she's been homeless for a while, which is likely why no one reported her missing. But we don't believe she was living in the woods at the time of her death."

"How sad, on multiple fronts." Elena pictured her in life, while unfortunately picturing her in death, as well. "Do you think she was a victim of the serial killer?"

"The timeline indicates that Hekekia was killed before Kakalina Kinoshita and Yancy Otani," he said, musing. "But the MO fits. When you add that with other elements of the case, I'd say that we're almost certainly talking about the work of the Big Island Killer. We just happened to miss discovering Hekekia's remains before the unsub could strike again."

Elena couldn't help but wonder how the perpetrator had been able to so easily slip between the fingers of law enforcement and the public, who were on guard against the attacker to the extent that they could be. Could there be more bodies out there, unknown and unclaimed, with the killer gloating?

Logan broke into her reverie when he said evenly, "There's been a break in the Big Island Killer investigation that will either give us what—and who—we're looking for or prove to be another disaster insofar as cracking the case."

"Tell me..." she urged him, feeling the strain he was under in dealing with an elusive monster on the Hawaiian island.

"Identifiable DNA has been pulled from the sledgehammer found near Hekekia's body. That's the good news." Logan's chin sagged. "Bad news is that it has been linked to a man who died by suicide six months ago. Now we're left to wonder if the DNA had been left over from when he was still alive. Or if he could have an identical twin brother, which we're looking into even as we speak."

"Wow!" Elena's gaze grew wide with wonder. "What are the odds of that happening?"

"Not very good," he allowed, raising his mug. "But stranger things have occurred. If this doesn't pan out with the brother, then the DNA will prove to be totally irrelevant to the murder of Kakalina Kinoshita, and the dead man, Mark Teale, can rest in peace. At least insofar as being involved in any way in this homicide."

Mark Teale, Elena repeated in her head. It rang a bell. But when and where? Then it registered. "I know that name… Mark Teale—" she practically shouted.

Logan cocked an eyebrow. "How?"

"Mark was a client."

"Really?" Logan leaned forward, his face intense. "Tell me more."

"He came to see me…about seven months ago," Elena recalled. "Mark was feeling depressed about his life. I knew he was troubled, but never expected it would reach the point of suicide." She tried tasting the coffee, but lost the desire to drink. "I only wish I had been able to better read the signs before it was too late, maybe recommend that he seek mental-health treatment beyond what I could give."

"Did Teale happen to mention anything about a twin brother?" Logan asked.

"No." Elena looked him in the eye contemplatively. "Mark said he had an identical twin sister named Marlene."

"Twin sister?" Logan repeated the words as though it had never dawned on him. "He used the term *identical* twin?"

"Yes," she said with certainty. "Mark claimed it was an anomaly, but true. According to him, it was Marlene who was the source of his problems. Apparently, she saw them as being tied at the hip, emotionally if not physically, and was clingy and controlling to the point that he simply couldn't take it anymore. Mark even claimed he had a girlfriend, whom he believed was in danger, given his sister's obsessive behavior. He felt trapped and didn't know where to turn."

"Hence, he came to see you?"

"Yes." Elena's eyes fell. "I did my best to help him. Obviously, it was not nearly enough."

"You can't blame yourself for the man taking his own life," Logan told her. "These things happen. Whatever hold Teale's sister had on him, it was powerful enough to make him want to check out rather than remain under her thumb."

It was a scary thought, but Elena knew Logan was right. Still, it left a sour taste in her mouth. "This is all so weird," she said.

"Yeah, I know." He rested his arm on the table. "Did you happen to meet the sister?"

"No. I did attend Mark's funeral and saw a tall, attractive woman dressed in black from a distance, but we never spoke." Elena paused. "I thought of offering my services as a grief counselor to help her deal with the loss, but somehow it didn't seem appropriate."

"Maybe not."

She eyed him. "How do you suppose Mark's DNA ended up on the sledgehammer?"

"Not sure it did," Logan remarked straightforwardly. "It's possible that because Teale and Paula Hekekia were both homeless at times, they could have intersected on that front. But that still doesn't tell us how his DNA would find its way to a murder weapon that connects Hekekia's death to a string of other murders of Hawaiian women."

"You think the DNA could have come from Marlene?" Elena asked, reading between the lines. "How's that even possible? Aren't true identical twins always of the same gender? Especially where it concerns a DNA match?"

"That's what I need to find out." Logan's voice lowered with fortitude. "Could be that we've been looking in the wrong direction all along in assuming that the Big Island Killer was a male."

"But why would Mark's sister go after these women?"

He shrugged. "Why does any serial killer kill? Maybe it was some form of sick obsession with her dead brother that somehow went too far in taking it out on those targeted. But before I get too carried away with theories, why don't we wait and see how this unfolds."

Elena nodded, restraining her own eagerness to get answers, putting her trust in him and the investigation. She rose. "You'd better get going."

"Yeah." Logan got to his feet. He put his hands on her shoulders and gazed down at her. "Keep your eyes open. If the sister is involved with these serial homicides, there's no telling how far she might go in her warped mind. That includes going after her brother's grief counselor."

Elena was chilled at the thought, but tried not

to show it. "I'll try to stay alert at all times," she promised.

"Okay." Logan kissed Elena on the mouth and they walked to her car, where they kissed again a little longer before she broke the lip-lock. They would have plenty of time to kiss and much more, once they were no longer under a cloud of murder and mayhem threatening to rain down on the entire island.

Chapter Sixteen

At the Hawaii Police Department's Scientific Investigation Section, Logan stood at the workstation of Shirley Takaki. He had tasked her with determining whether or not the DNA extracted from the sledgehammer found at the Waiākea Forest Reserve crime scene could possibly belong to Mark Teale's supposed identical twin sister, Marlene, since they didn't have an actual sample of her DNA.

"Well, what have you learned?" Logan pressed his lips together, wondering if this was a wild-goose chase—trying to link a serial murder case to a blood relative of a deceased suspect for whom the DNA lined up. "Give me something we can work with."

"I think I can, to one degree or another." Shirley smiled as she sat at a laminate-top science table in an ergonomic lab chair. She glanced at her laptop and back. "I've been doing some research and have found that virtually all cases of identical twins are the same sex. Or to put it another way, in 99.9

percent of boy-girl twins, they are nonidentical or dizygotic twins."

Logan didn't like those odds one bit, yet he had to believe there was a method to the madness that could still add up in their search for a killer.

Shirley moved hair from her face. "But here's the rub—in very rare instances, a genetic mutation can occur in which identical twins develop from an egg and sperm that started out as males, in which they shared the XY chromosomes, before losing a copy of the dominant Y chromosome in changing into a male-female pair. The condition is known as Turner syndrome."

"So you're telling me that it's actually possible that a female can be the identical twin to a male and carry the same DNA?" Logan asked, while wrapping his mind around the notion.

Shirley hesitated. "Yes, I believe this is a possibility based on what I've just outlined," she explained, "in relation to the DNA found on the sledgehammer that's mostly likely not from the deceased Mark Teale. Of course, the only way to know for certain is to get a DNA sample from his sister and see if we can match it to the crime-scene DNA profiles."

"That, we can do," he said confidently, knowing that a judge would likely sign off on a search warrant. But first, they needed to locate this Marlene, wherever she might be, as a potentially dangerous and unstable serial killer.

An hour later, Logan had assembled members of

the task force into the conference room to discuss this latest twist in the Big Island Killer investigation. He allowed Shirley to present her findings on the DNA evidence and its relationship to a deceased suspect and his twin sister, before Ivy spoke. "I was able to dig up some interesting information on Marlene Teale, the identical sibling of Mark Teale. Seems as though the thirty-four-year-old Ms. Teale has been in and out of mental institutions for much of her life with various personality disorders and anger-management issues. She was last hospitalized two years ago for psychiatric evaluation after threatening the life of her brother, Mark, who had taken out a restraining order against her."

Ivy pointed the remote at the large format display, bringing up an image. "This is what Marlene Teale looked like at the time." Logan regarded the suspect, who was average-looking, with an angular face surrounded by a short, choppy blond hairstyle with side bangs. She wore glasses and had blue eyes. He wondered if this could actually be the face of a serial monster.

"Ms. Teale's last known address was on Pulima Drive," Ivy continued. "With any luck, she still lives there and we can pay her a little visit. Or track down the Chrysler Pacifica registered to the suspect."

"While we're at it," Logan added unsmilingly, "we can compel her through a search warrant to give a sample of her DNA, assuming she won't supply it voluntarily. Then see what else she may be hiding relevant to our investigation."

"The idea that this Marlene Teale is our serial killer, based on shaky forensic evidence, is a bit of a stretch, don't you think?" Aretha asked dubiously.

Logan faced her, expecting that he would get some pushback on the theory yet to be substantiated, all things considered. But his gut instincts, combined with the unusual nature of the DNA analysis, told him they were onto something. Now he only needed to back this up with hard evidence. "What I think, Agent Kennedy, is that we've had one dead end after another. As long as this one is still possible, if not necessarily plausible, we'll work with it and see what happens."

She relented. "You're the lead investigator, Detective Ryder. With the deaths mounting, if you can thread the needle and stick it in the newest suspect, go for it."

"Appreciate that." He nodded, acknowledging her tacit support. Eyeing her former FBI mate and former criminal profiler Georgina Machado, he asked curiously, "Care to weigh in?"

"Sure." She smiled, then observed the picture of the suspect still occupying the screen. "It's quite a fascinating prospect of an identical female twin of a dead male being the Big Island Killer, based on slipping up and leaving controversial DNA evidence. The long odds notwithstanding, far be it for me to rule this out. On the contrary, in spite of the fact that males are predominately more likely to be serial killers, females are still well represented in the annals as serial killers. We're talking about Martha Beck, Rosemary West, Judy Buenoano, Charlene Gallego, Karla Homolka... Shall I go on? Be it profit, jealousy, obsession, revenge, hatred—you name it—women have all the same excuses as men and can be just as deadly. Let's see if Marlene Teale is a red herring. Or a cold-blooded killer just waiting for us to finally figure it out and take her into custody."

"That's good enough for me," Logan told her respectfully. It had better be, he knew, given that the stakes were never higher for ending the state of terror inflicted upon the citizens of Hilo. With Hawaiian women on the front lines of danger.

Ivy got his attention when she announced on cue, "We've got the warrant to go after Marlene Teale."

"Let's not waste any time," Logan responded decisively as they moved into action.

"HMM... I THOUGHT I recognized the name Mark Teale," Ivy said from the passenger seat as she rode with Logan. She was holding a tablet computer.

"What do you have?" Logan glanced at her while driving.

"Seems as though Teale's name came up when we were investigating the death of Liann Nahuina, the first identified victim of the Big Island Killer. Apparently, the two had been cohabitating before

Teale's suicide, which resulted in us taking him off the list of suspects."

"Interesting." Logan's mind was churning. "Wonder if there's some symmetry between the two deaths? A cause and effect, if you will?"

"You mean as in the twin sister of Teale going after Nahuina in some sort of misguided attempt at revenge or unnatural grief over his death?"

"Why not?" Logan mulled over the notion. "Sounds far-fetched, but no more so than different-sex twins sharing the same DNA, one of which left some on the sledgehammer used to kill Paula Hekekia."

"True." Ivy took a breath. "But if Nahuina was the primary target of Marlene Teale, why kill the other women?"

"Maybe because of the similar features," Logan said, and thought of Elena, who had the same traits as an attractive Hawaiian female. "Or just to throw us off."

"If so, she succeeded," Ivy argued. "And if not, we've still got a devious unsub on the loose."

"We'll find out soon enough." Logan only wished it had come before Paula Hekekia was murdered, only to have Elena go through the trauma of discovering the body. He sensed that her fortitude as a grief counselor had played a big role in allowing her to better process the experience. That didn't mean she wasn't still in harm's way, with the killer yet to be taken into custody.

He brought the car to a stop on Pulima Drive and they got out. The bungalow-style residence sat on a corner lot with a few bamboo palm and rambutan trees dotting the landscape. A carport was empty, making Logan believe the occupant was not present. But taking no chances, the team, including Agent Kennedy, was armed and ready should they encounter a threat or any resistance. With his Glock pistol out, he led the way, with Aretha and Ivy on his heels. They would request backup, if needed. Stepping onto the lanai, Logan listened for any sounds coming from within. Hearing none, he banged on the door and announced their presence, mindful that the suspect was still innocent until proven guilty.

When no one answered after repeated knocks, the order was given to break the door open using a Halligan tool, after which Logan barreled inside, unsure what they might find, but sensing it would be some answers. They fanned out across the driftwood flooring of the cottage-like home with an open floor plan. It was sparsely furnished. A mildew scent permeated the air, as if the place hadn't been lived in much of late. Logan wondered if the suspect still lived in the house. Or was someone else occupying it?

"We're clear," Ivy shouted, indicating that there were no threats to their safety inside.

Logan put away his firearm as he continued to make his way around, when he heard Aretha make a cryptic comment. "You may want to take a look at this, Ryder."

He followed her voice to the master bedroom, where the FBI agent was hovering by the closet. "What have you got?"

"What haven't we got is more like it?" Aretha motioned him over, as Logan noted that below the ceiling fan, the full-size bed was made. A large window, facing the backyard, was closed, making it even stuffier inside. "Looks as though someone has been stockpiling the tools of the Big Island Killer in here…"

He gazed into the closet and Logan saw aluminum baseball bats, wooden mallets, lava rock, lead pipes and sledgehammers—all of which had been used to murder five women with blunt-force trauma. His eyes widened with shock. "Guess we've come to the right place," he muttered humorlessly, even if they hadn't confirmed that it was occupied by Marlene Teale. "No wonder the perp didn't bother to collect the murder weapons, knowing there were plenty more where those came from."

"Meaning that the killer was just getting started," Aretha said grimly. "Unless we stood in the way, no telling how many more women would be targeted."

"I wouldn't want to even speculate," Logan said, frowning at the mere thought, with Elena in mind. "We need to get Forensics here in a hurry." He believed that, aside from the treasure trove of circumstantial evidence, there should be DNA evidence that would link the occupant to the DNA found on the sledgehammer that killed Paula Hekekia.

"I found something." The sound of urgency in Ivy's voice got Logan's attention. They followed her to a second room, where she said, "From the looks of it, Marlene Teale still lives here, at least part of the time. More disturbing is what the lady's been up to and who she's now targeting…"

Logan gazed ■ a white wooden L-shaped desk against the wall. On it was a photograph of Mark and Marlene Teale that looked to have been taken in the last year or so. Next to it on one side were pictures of the Big Island Killer victims: Liann Nahuina, Daryl Renigado, Yancy Otani, Kakalina Kinoshita and Paula Hekekia. Each face had an *X* across it, as if to indicate elimination; along with premeditation in staking out the victims beforehand. Logan inhaled a sharp breath, as his eyes turned to the other side of the center photo of the identical twins and saw the picture of Elena. There was no *X* on it, but the fact that she was there at all told him that the killer was planning to hunt her down and kill her.

"Elena's next on Teale's list," Ivy said, a catch in her voice, but he'd already figured it out.

"I have to warn her." Logan's heart pounded in his ears, knowing the woman he had fallen in love with—and he was ready to admit it—was now in danger for her life.

"With Marlene Teale being the Big Island Killer and apparently mad as a hatter," Aretha began, "we need to move fast to find her before she can get to her next target."

Ivy nodded in agreement, getting out her cell phone. "We'll issue a BOLO alert for Teale and the Chrysler Pacifica she's driving."

With his own phone, Logan took a picture of Marlene Teale's face to send to Elena, so she would be aware and could avoid the dangerous woman at all costs. Until such time, they would place Elena in protective custody, to keep her safe and sound, so long as Teale remained on the loose. Assuming it wasn't too late.

ELENA LEFT THE office to wait in her car for Tommy to show up. They would ride together to have lunch at a seafood restaurant in Downtown Hilo, at which time he planned to tell her about his newest adventure as a tour guide. She was happy to see him try to get on with his life, following the death of Kakalina. Elena knew there would still be good and bad days, but felt that time would lessen the blow and allow him to return to some semblance of normalcy. Just as had been the case for her after Errol's passing. She had managed to get beyond the grieving and find a new love. *Did I just say* love? Elena asked herself, repeating the word in her head. Even if the thought was a little scary and she was unsure if Logan felt the same way, the heart knew what the heart knew. She did love Logan Ryder and would have to muster up the guts to tell him.

Just as Elena opened the door to her car, she felt a presence behind her. Turning around, her initial fear of an attacker was abated somewhat when she recognized the person. It was Marybeth Monaghan, one of her clients. "Hi, Marybeth," she said politely.

Marybeth gave her a friendly smile. "Hey."

Elena lifted her eyes curiously. "Did we have an appointment for today?"

"Not really." She touched her glasses demurely. "I was still having some issues and decided I'd take a chance that you'd be around."

"I'm sorry, but I have a lunch date, so…" Elena hated to disappoint her, but she didn't want to cancel getting together with her brother, feeling it was important that they do what was needed to strengthen their own bond after recent challenges. Surely, Marybeth would understand? When her cell phone rang, Elena lifted it from her pocket and saw that the caller was Logan. Her heart skipped a beat at being able to hear his voice. She sensed, though, that the call could be an important update on the case instead of what she meant to him. Glancing at her client, Elena said softly, "Excuse me, but I have to get this…"

Marybeth gave a halfhearted smile, but did not budge. Suddenly feeling uneasy for some reason, Elena turned away from her and answered the phone. "Hey," she uttered.

"Mark Teale's sister is the Big Island Killer," Logan said in a panicked tone. "Her name is Marlene Teale and I think she's coming after you."

"Really?" Elena's fear radar shot up at the prospect of being in the crosshairs of a serial killer. Even if she had no idea why, other than that she resembled the other victims.

"Yes," he snapped urgently. "I'm sending you a picture of her. If you see this woman anywhere, stay away from her until I can get there…"

When she got the photo, Elena stared at a face she recognized, save for the different shade of hair. Marlene Teale *was* Marybeth Monaghan, the woman standing behind her. Before she could react and reveal to Logan that she was in serious trouble, Elena felt something slam against the side of her head. Without even realizing it, she blacked out, not knowing if she would ever get the chance to express her true feelings to Logan.

Chapter Seventeen

Elena opened her eyes with a splitting headache. What happened? Where was she? How did she get there? Then it began to come back to her, groggy as she was. She had been hit hard on the head by someone. But who? She strained to remember, before it clicked like a light bulb flashing in her brain. She had been assaulted by Marlene Teale, the woman Elena knew as Marybeth Monaghan. Only it had been an alias to hide her true identity as the sister of Elena's former, and now dead, client, Mark Teale. And, according to Logan, a serial killer.

It took another moment or two for Elena to realize that she was bleeding on the side of her head— the warm blood had trickled down her left ear and cheek onto her neck. She further recognized that she was seated on a wooden cross-back chair with her hands tied behind her back with rope. *Where has she taken me?* Elena pondered worriedly. Clearing her vision, she saw that she was near a cottage-style beige-colored wall in a small living room with gray laminate wood flooring and an open concept. The place was lightly furnished with rustic reclaimed barnwood furniture. Double-hung windows were covered by faux-wood plantation blinds, with the source of illumination a small vintage glass lamp that was sitting on a three-sided cream-colored corner table.

As she assessed the situation, Elena tried to wrest her hands free with no luck. She had to get out of there. Alert Logan that she was in peril. Or was he already looking for her and trying to rescue her? Along with trying to take down a stone-cold killer? But how on earth would he know where to look? Something told Elena that her kidnapper had taken her somewhere not easily found. But for what purpose, other than to kill her with a slow, torturous death?

When the front door burst open and her abductor entered, carrying a black duffel bag, Elena wondered if she should pretend to still be unconscious or not. She opted for the latter, figuring that Marlene Teale was not likely to fall for it.

"So you're finally awake." Marlene dropped the bag on the floor and walked up to Elena with an amused look playing on her lips. "Sorry about the conk on the head." She laughed mockingly. "Actually, I'm not. Unfortunately for you, I'm not done with you yet. By the time I am, believe me, you'll be glad when it's over, because you'll be dead."

I have to say something to this seriously disturbed lady, Elena told herself, trying her best to remain calm. "Why are you doing this, Marybeth?" she asked, pretending to still only know her by her fake name. "What have I ever done to you, but try and help?"

"Save the act, okay?" Marlene narrowed her eyes behind the glasses. "I know you know my real name's Marlene Teale. I saw the picture of me your cop boyfriend sent to your cell phone. He's on to me and, I'm sure, what I've been up to. But that won't help you at all. While you were snoozing, I got rid of your cell phone so it can't be used to track your location. No one knows you're here. It's my secret hideaway, so don't count on being rescued by him or anyone else."

Realizing it was not going to do her any good playing dumb, Elena felt that the next best thing was to try to get some answers out of her while stalling for time. "Yes, I know you're Mark Teale's identical twin, Marlene," she confessed. "What I don't understand is why you would want to hurt me? I did everything I could to help Mark. It wasn't my fault that he took his own life."

"Is that what you think?" Marlene laughed hysterically. "If you want to know the truth—and it doesn't matter at this point, since you'll never live to tell a soul—Mark didn't kill himself."

Elena's eyebrows cocked in surprise, notwithstanding the threat to her own life. "What?"

"I only made it look like he had," she said, bragging. "My brother wanted to cut off all ties to me, as if I meant nothing to him anymore. Can you believe he actually fell in love with someone, or so he claimed, for the first time in his life? Her name was Liann Nahuina. After all I did for him, we were supposed to always be there for each other. Have each other's backs, through thick and thin. Then he wants to kick me, his twin sister, to the curb—for what, her? I couldn't let that happen. So I put on a convincing act to get him to meet me at the park to say our goodbyes, where I used a gun stolen from my married former lover and shot Mark in the head. I put the gun in his hand to make it look like it was self-inflicted. Everyone believed it. I hated to lose the only person who truly got me, but he made me do it."

She really is unhinged and obviously homicidal with jealous rage in a sibling-attachment way, Elena told herself, shuddering at the thought that she had murdered her own twin brother as if it was just a walk in the park. *Who does that?* Elena wondered what else she could get her kidnapper to reveal that could later be used against her. Now that the cat was out of the proverbial bag, there was no reason for her kidnapper to deny who and what she was. "What about those poor women? Did you kill them, too, as the Big Island Killer? And, if so, why?"

Marlene hardened her face. "Yes, I killed them, like I'm going to kill you," she replied tartly. "Why? The first one, Liann, was Mark's girlfriend and the reason he turned against me. She needed to pay for that. She made it easy to take her life away, living off the grid as she did, in this very cottage…"

Elena scanned the place again, as she mulled over this revelation. Could Logan possibly figure out that this was where she had been taken? Or was Marlene right in that there was no escape from her maniacal plan to kill her?

"The others were meant to throw the police off any possible trail to me," Marlene continued, as if proud of herself and the deception. "The fact that Liann happened to be Hawaiian, it wasn't that difficult to locate some other Hawaiian women with similar features to dispose of. I decided to kill each of them with a different object to confuse the authorities even more. But the funny thing is, I started to feel good about it with each killing. I came to realize that I liked having the power to take away lives. It seemed like killing was in my blood. Too bad it took killing Mark to make me realize this." She paused, as if a flicker of regret hit her. Then the steely cold countenance returned. "But I'm just getting started. The Big Island Killer, as they chose to name me, has more tricks up her sleeve in targeting others who don't look like Liann. That will really confound the police as a wickedly clever serial killer."

"What do you want from me?" Elena had hesitated to ask, even as she continued to try in vain to break her hands free. Why hadn't she killed her already? *Or do I really want to know?* Elena thought. "Why the ruse in pretending to be Marybeth Monaghan?"

"The Marybeth part was simply a way to get to you without giving myself away. After I learned that Mark went to you for counseling, I wanted to see for myself who it was that he poured his heart out to. Though I lied about my mother passing away recently, she really did die from pancreatic cancer—only when Mark and I were six years old. Without a father ever in the picture, we were then placed in foster care." Marlene sighed, sadness in her eyes, but her face hardened once again. "Imagine how surprised I was to discover that you bore a strong resemblance to Liann. It was almost too perfect as someone who had interfered with the kinship I had with my brother. I knew then that it was only a matter of time before you would die, too. That time is near and there's absolutely nothing you can do about it—"

Elena fought hard not to believe her chilling words, which made any possibility of getting out of her predicament seem hopeless. Dying before reaching the age of thirty-three, before having a chance to have a life with Logan, wasn't what she'd bargained for. Certainly not at the hands of a mentally unstable, but still quite capable, serial murderer. "Just let me go and I won't tip the police off." She doubted her kidnapper would buy that, but wanted to make it sound believable, anyhow.

Marlene crouched down so their faces were lined up and inches apart. "Sorry, but no can do," she growled. "You have to die like the others. Mark would want that, too. After all, he chose to bring you into the picture that, as his identical twin, made me a part of it, as well. The only reason you're still breathing, with probably a massive headache, is because you're a grief counselor and I wanted to get some final therapy of sorts in memory of my brother, as a parting shot to your demise."

Elena swallowed the lump in her throat, as she had to come to terms with the reality that her abductor seemed to hold all the cards. Meaning that her life hung in the balance. Unless she could find a way to prevent Marlene from carrying out her plans to murder her.

LOGAN GOT A bad feeling in his gut when Elena's phone suddenly went dead in the middle of their conversation. Had it been merely a lost signal? Or something more ominous? Such as Marlene Teale getting to her before they could pick up the armed and dangerous suspect in the murder of five women. Before he could wrap his mind around the unsettling possibilities, Logan got a call from Elena's brother.

"Hey, I'm standing in the parking lot next to Elena's car outside the office complex where she works," Tommy said, concern evident in his tone. "We were supposed to get together for lunch. Only she's not here, but her car door is open..."

"Did you try calling her cell phone?" Logan strained not to panic. "Maybe Elena forgot something in her office."

"Yes, I called her. There was no answer." Tommy's

voice cracked. "I'm freaking out here, thinking that something bad may have happened to my sister."

I'm thinking the same thing, Logan told himself, but had to keep it together for both their sakes. "Let's not jump to conclusions," he said evenly. He had to believe that Elena was still alive, whatever the case. "Maybe there's an explanation as to why she isn't there. Hang tight, I'm on my way. In the meantime, keep trying to reach her and don't touch the car. It may now be an official crime scene."

"Okay." Tommy hung up and Logan was left with a sense of dread as he turned to the others at the bungalow where Marlene Teale had been staying. "I think Teale may have Elena." He explained why, while resisting the more morbid thoughts that if the serial killer suspect had kidnapped Elena in broad daylight, her chances for survival were bleak, at best.

"If she does," Ivy told him steadfastly, "we'll find her."

"One can only hope." Logan refused to think otherwise. Now that he had found Elena as a woman he had a future with, losing her to the Big Island Killer was not an option as long as there was an ounce of breath in him.

"With the BOLO out, we're in full pursuit of Teale," Aretha reminded him. "She no longer has the element of surprise on her side. Or maybe places that she can go."

"I know," he said solemnly. "That's what I'm afraid of. If Teale feels cornered, there's no telling what she's capable of." He considered that she might try to use Elena as a bargaining chip to get away. That was assuming the twin sister of Mark Teale hadn't already harmed Elena, given her MO. "I'm heading over to the parking lot where Elena apparently was abducted. Send a forensic team over there to look for evidence. Also, let's see if we can use cell site location information and GPS data to triangulate the location of Elena's cell phone." Even in seeking the information, Logan suspected that if Elena had been kidnapped, her abductor would likely have disposed of the evidence near the point of abduction. Still, they had to exercise every means to locate her, as Elena's life depended on it with every excruciating second counting.

"I'll get on it," Ivy assured him. "And we'll check parks, trails, woods, vacant fields, anywhere Teale could have taken her."

"Good." Logan knew he could count on her and the entire PD and FBI to do everything in their power to try to prevent another human being from being murdered by the Big Island Killer. But would any of that be enough to save Elena?

He raced to the scene of Elena's disappearance, and spotted Tommy pacing in the parking lot of the office complex on Waianuenue Avenue. Logan pulled up near Elena's Subaru Outback and got out. He winced, picturing her being accosted by a killer and how terrifying it must have been to be in that situation. Adding to his uneasiness, he saw what seemed to be drops of blood just outside the car. Elena's? Apparently, Tommy had failed to notice it. Probably a good thing, Logan believed. He hoped Elena was strong enough to withstand whatever Teale dished out until he could get to her.

"Did you check Elena's office?" Logan asked her brother.

"Yeah. It was locked and no sign she was inside."

"I doubt she was," Logan admitted sourly.

"What's going on?" Tommy narrowed his eyes agitatedly. "What aren't you telling me?"

Locking eyes with him, Logan responded straightforwardly, "We think Elena may have been abducted."

"By who?"

While hating to spill out the words, given the obvious implications, Logan felt that Elena's brother needed to know the seriousness of the situation that they were up against. "The Big Island Killer."

The color seemed to drain from Tommy's face and Logan could almost read his mind. First Kakalina Kinoshita. And now Elena. "Are you saying that this serial killer has Elena and has murdered her…?"

"I'm saying that neither of us should panic at this point," Logan told him, while trying hard to practice what he was preaching. "Until we know for sure, we have to assume that Elena is still alive."

Tommy went stone-cold silent as the crime-scene technicians arrived. Logan insisted that Elena's brother go home and wait until there was news, or in case she miraculously showed up. He complied begrudgingly and Logan went to the office complex's security office to get a look at the parking-lot surveillance video. The security coordinator, Diego Holokai, in his sixties and bald-headed, wasted little time in pulling up the video with the sense of urgency attached to it by Logan.

"Okay, let's see what we've got," Diego said.

Logan watched as the video slowed down and zoomed in to when Elena stood by her car talking to a woman he recognized as Marlene Teale. The way Elena was conversing with her, it appeared as though they were not strangers. Could the killer have gone undercover as a client in order to get a read on her target beforehand? Logan saw Elena turn away and talk on her cell phone—presumably to him. It was after he sent the picture of the suspect that Elena was hit in the head by Marlene with what appeared to be a piece of lava rock.

"What the…?" Diego's voice cracked in disbelief.

Logan cringed in horror as Elena seemed to lose consciousness right away. He only wished he had been able to reach her five minutes earlier, kicking himself at the timing misfortune. Before she could fall to the ground, Elena was caught by Marlene and dragged out of view. "Pan the video out," Logan ordered, needing to see where the kidnapper took her.

"You've got it," the security coordinator said, complying.

Peering, Logan saw that Marlene was now wearing a dark hoodie over her head as she tossed Elena into the passenger seat of a silver Chrysler Pacifica, matching the one registered to the suspect. Then Marlene ran around the vehicle, got behind the wheel and took off. It was obvious to him that she had planned this in advance and, frighteningly, it had gone off without a hitch.

Diego frowned. "Where is she taking her and why?"

"Have no idea on the first question." Logan hated to admit it, feeling helpless in his quest to avert another tragedy. "As to the why, she's a serial killer and is planning to commit murder—if we can't find her."

"I hope you do," he said sincerely.

The clock was ticking, Logan thought miserably, knowing that if he didn't get to Elena soon, she was as good as dead. "I need a copy of that video. I'll send someone to pick it up later."

"No problem."

Logan left him to get back to the search for the woman he intended to ask to marry him, if he ever got that chance. After conferring with detectives on the scene in what had become an active case of kidnapping, Logan climbed back in his car, not able to stand idle while Elena was out there somewhere alone with a madwoman and serial killer, with Elena unsure if she would survive her ordeal or not. *I'll never stop trying to find you as long as there's any possibility you're still alive*, he thought to himself.

When his cell phone rang, Logan answered, putting it on speaker. "The car Teale's driving was spotted a little while ago on Komohana Street heading toward South Hilo," Ivy informed him. "We've dispatched all available vehicles to the area."

A bell suddenly rang in Logan's head. "Wasn't the cottage where Liann Nahuina's body found off of Komohana Street?"

"Yes, I believe so," Ivy confirmed. "Why do you ask?"

"Call it a hunch," he told her thoughtfully, "but the off-the-grid cottage seems like the perfect place for Teale to operate and lay low as the last location her brother called home, at least part-time, before his death."

"You could be right about that."

"Only one way to find out," Logan said, pressing his foot down on the accelerator. "I'm not far from there." If his instincts were correct, he didn't have a second to spare.

"I'll alert the SWAT unit and head over there myself with Aretha and other reinforcements," Ivy stated decisively.

"I was counting on that." He disconnected, not about to wait for backup. Not this time. Not when Elena meant far too much to him to depend on anyone to come to her rescue but himself. If Marlene had kept her alive, it wouldn't be for long. But maybe just long enough, Logan believed, to do whatever he needed to neutralize the threat and make sure Elena was safe and sound.

He drove the car to the side of the road, just far enough from the cottage to not announce his arrival to the kidnapper. Stepping outside, where it had started to rain, Logan removed the firearm from his pocket holster and approached the location he believed Elena had been taken to. He moved silently across a brown field and spotted a silver Chrysler Pacifica parked in the back. The license plate number corresponded with the vehicle registered to Marlene Teale, giving more credence to Logan's belief that Elena was there.

With his gun drawn, Logan checked for any signs of her in the vehicle. Seeing none, he approached the side of the cottage, careful not to tip his hand, not knowing if the suspect had a firearm or not. He wasn't willing to take any unnecessary chances when it came to Elena's life. Gazing inside a dirty side window while ignoring the rain pelting his face, he could see Elena sitting in a chair. Her hands appeared to be bound. At first, there was no movement and he feared the worst. But then she jerked her head and seemed to say something. *She's alive*, he thought, feeling a sudden adrenaline rush to make sure Elena stayed that way.

Logan's vision turned toward the kidnapper, who was hovering over Elena like a mighty conqueror enjoying her position of power. She didn't appear to have a gun in her possession. But even if she wasn't packing, he didn't doubt that she had other potentially deadly weapons within reach, as Logan thought of the lava rock used to assault Elena. Not to mention the cache of lethal items found in the closet of Teale's residence, similar to the ones used to murder five women. Marlene clearly planned to kill Elena, perhaps after extracting information from her. *Not if I can help it*, Logan thought, ready to make his move to avert disaster.

"YOU DON'T HAVE to do this," Elena pleaded with her kidnapper, hoping to buy time, if nothing else, as she heard the rainfall. She sensed that Logan was out there somewhere near, doing his best to extricate her from the desperate situation she was in. In the meantime, Elena had finally begun to feel the rope loosening, but still not enough to break free.

"I'm afraid I do," Marlene taunted her. "I need to finish this for Mark. The sibling bond between us is unbroken, even with his death. I should think you of all people would understand this. You have your own sibling bond. It's Tommy, isn't it?" Elena reacted to the familiarity with her brother. Marlene made a snickering sound, as if pleased with herself. "Yeah, thought so. You know, I didn't realize he was your brother when I followed him and the lady from the club. I thought I might have to go against the grain and kill her inside her house, along with anyone else who got in the way. But then Tommy let her out of the car and she was only too happy to hitch a ride with me, drunk as Kakalina was. I doubt she ever realized what was happening to her, until it was much too late. Never considered that your brother might be taken into custody for the crime. Lucky for him that I wasn't about to let Tommy take credit for what I was doing. If the police hadn't released him, I might've had to come after you sooner. Then your cop boyfriend would have realized too little, too late, that they had the wrong person under lock and key."

"You're sick," Elena uttered contemptuously, feeling queasy at the thought that she might already be dead, never to see Logan or Tommy again, had it not been for a twist of fate. She only wished someone else didn't have to die in the interim.

"I suppose I am," Marlene admitted, a delirious chuckle cracking through the air. She halted it on a dime. "But sane enough to finish what I started in killing you. Unlike the others, though, out of the goodness of my heart—or maybe to make it sporting—you'll get the choice of how you're to die…" She went to the duffel bag and removed several items, including an aluminum baseball bat, lava rock, lead pipe, wooden mallet and a sledgehammer. She laid them out on the floor, as if on display. "Pick one," she demanded.

"I can't," Elena choked out, not wanting to play her insane and evil game.

"Do it!" Marlene's voice echoed venomously throughout the room. "Otherwise, I'll do it for you and, just maybe, choose two of them to attack you with—one to start, the other to finish—"

So, this is it, Elena thought resignedly, twisting

her hands every which way frantically to get them loose, while frightened beyond belief. Not so much in dying before her time. But in not getting the chance to say goodbye to Logan, the love of her life. And Tommy, the only relative she had left. She couldn't go down without a fight. Elena finally freed her hands, knowing she had only one shot to get out of this alive. She uttered submissively, "How about the lava rock?" She sensed that was what the serial killer had used to hit her on the head in the parking lot.

"Good choice." Marlene laughed maniacally. "Might have chosen the same myself, had I been in your situation. Especially considering the alternatives."

When she turned to the killing tools, Elena sprang up, catching Marlene off guard. "I won't become another victim of yours."

"Oh really?" Marlene quickly overcame her surprise that Elena had freed herself. "We'll see about that." She grabbed the lead pipe and approached her. "Guess I've been left to make the choice for you in how you'll die…" She swung the pipe, hitting nothing but air.

Elena's blood ran hot as she dodged the attempt to hit her in the head. Putting her kickboxing skills to the test, she raised her leg and landed a hard kick to Marlene's face, knocking the serial killer off balance. The woman yelled an expletive, shook off the pain, regained her balance and again swung the pipe at Elena's head, but she managed to avert it with

quick foot action. In the blink of an eye in a coun-
termove, she brought her leg up and kicked Marlene
solidly in the pit of her stomach, and in the same motion put a foot solidly to the side of the kidnapper's
head. Marlene's glasses flew from her face as she
staggered and shrieked.

Feeling as though she was gaining the upper hand,
Elena's pulse raced as she lifted both feet off the
ground. She struck her assailant's face with one foot,
knocking the pipe out of her hands as Marlene fell
hard to the floor, before Elena landed back on her
feet firmly. Just as it appeared as if it was over and
she was victorious, Marlene grabbed the sledgehammer, rose and started to charge Elena with a crazed
look in her eyes.

Backpedaling, Elena lost her balance and fell onto
the floor. Her heart beating wildly, she struggled to
stand, fearing that if Marlene got on top of her, the
serial killer would do as she intended in bludgeoning her to death as another victim of the Big Island
Killer. The front door suddenly burst open and Elena
watched in amazement as Logan barreled in, his gun
aimed squarely at Marlene.

"Drop it!" His voice was commanding. "I said,
drop it, Marlene. It's over. Now!"

The murderer's features contorted like a rabid animal, as Marlene turned away from her and faced
Logan. Instead of obeying the detective's order, she
charged at him with the sledgehammer as if she had

nothing to lose, and Logan fired one shot, then another, before the serial killer went down.

Bypassing the unconscious Marlene, Elena rushed toward Logan, who put his gun away with the threat brought under control, and wrapped her arms tightly around his neck, almost wishing they could remain that way forever. "That was a very close call," she said, catching her breath. "Thanks for showing up just in time."

"Nice to see you, too," he said wryly, holding her closely in his arms. She could feel the wetness on his body from the rain. "You're bleeding," he noted with concern.

Only then did Elena remember the pop on the side of her head and the fact that there was blood coming from the gash. "Nothing I can't overcome with a few stitches, a hot shower and a good night's sleep."

"Good." Logan kissed her temple. "Kickboxing, huh?" His voice was tinged with amusement. "I caught some of the action through the window before I came in."

She blushed. "It has its moments."

"I can see that."

Elena released her hold on his neck and gazed into Logan's unblinking eyes with curiosity. "How did you find me?"

"Teale's car was spotted in the area," Logan explained. "I had a feeling that she might have been using the vacant and out-of-the-way cottage her brother shared with Liann Nahuina before his death as a place to hide out…and, apparently, perpetrate more violent crime."

Elena felt a drop in her blood pressure as she turned to the fallen serial killer and back. "She killed him…"

Logan's right eyebrow shot up. "What?"

"Marlene confessed to murdering Mark in some sort of jealous-sibling spat that morphed into homicidal revenge," Elena told him. "She made it look like suicide."

"Why am I not surprised?" Logan took an exaggerated sigh. "Especially given the odd twists and turns of their symbiotic relationship as identical twins." His forehead creased. "Too bad she felt the need to go after and murder five innocent women in the aftermath."

"That's a whole different story." Elena mused about her own harrowing experience at the hands of Marlene and how much different the outcome could have been, considering the victims who didn't pull through.

Logan seemed to read her mind and, staring deep into her eyes, said in earnest, "Fortunately, we were able to draw the line there. If something had happened to you that there was no coming back from, I would never have been able to truly tell you how I feel."

Her heart skipped a beat. "And just how do you feel?"

"I'm in love with you, Elena," he said plainly,

"and I'd like you to become my wife and mother to as many children as you'd like."

She put her hands to her mouth as the powerful words registered in her ears. It was just what she wanted to hear and, for a little while there, she'd feared she might never have been afforded the opportunity. "I'd love to marry you, Logan." She minced no words in expressing how she truly felt about him. "Especially since I've fallen in love with you, too. And I can think of no better way to show it than by becoming your wife and the mother to as many children as we decide to bring into this world."

"Mahalo." Logan beamed ecstatically. "Shall we seal the deal with a kiss?"

Elena laughed. "I'd be pretty disappointed if we didn't."

"So would I." On that note, he slanted his face just right and gave her a passionate kiss that had Elena seeing stars. Something told her Logan was seeing them as well, as they planted the seeds for a lifetime together, built on love, trust, respect, adventure… and, yes, parenthood in paradise.

Epilogue

Six months later, Mr. and Mrs. Logan Ryder were walking hand in hand on a sunny afternoon along the black sand beach at Hilo Bayfront Beach Park on Kamehameha Avenue, a popular park just a short distance from downtown Hilo. They were celebrating their two-month anniversary as husband and wife, leaving Elena still breathless and overjoyed to have found her soul mate and second love of her life in the handsome detective. Not wanting to wait to begin their union, she had moved into his house two weeks after Logan proposed to her, prompted by his urging and promise to do whatever was necessary to make it their home. Instead of putting her own house on the market, while holding onto the precious memories of her life there, Elena offered the place instead to Tommy at a bargain price. He gleefully accepted, while turning the *ohana* into a rental property.

"What's happening in that pretty little head of yours?" Logan asked, breaking into her daydreaming with interest.

"Oh, just thinking about what a difference half a year can make," she told him musingly, while staring at the murky waters of Hilo Bay with the ocean as the backdrop. "I feel as if a great weight has been lifted off our shoulders, allowing us the opportunity to recalibrate."

"Yeah, one's whole world can change in a short time." He held her hand tighter. "For the better, I might add."

"Definitely." Elena beamed, rejoicing in their blissful relationship and exciting plans to add to their family. But then she thought about those who were less fortunate. Specifically, the six murdered victims of Marlene Teale, the woman who gained infamy as the Big Island Killer. She had survived her injuries and was currently in jail, while showing no signs of remorse. Including the killing of her own twin brother. Elena couldn't imagine doing such a thing to Tommy, no matter how great their differences. But if there was a silver lining to Mark's death, it was that he didn't take his own life as had originally been thought. Elena felt relieved that this also meant she needn't bear any guilt that she could have played a role in his suicide as a counselor. On the other hand, she certainly could not have conceived that Mark's obsessed sister would not only murder him, but also come after her for merely trying to help him and happening to look like his girlfriend. Elena raised her eyes pensively to meet Logan's. "So what's going to happen to Marlene?"

"That will be left for the courts to decide." He flashed a look of frustration. "Right now, the lawyers and psychiatrists are sparring over her competency to stand trial. Who knows how long that will take? The PD and task force did our job in identifying and apprehending the kidnapper and serial killer. The rest is out of our hands. As of now, Teale's sanity is in serious doubt, given the unnatural attachment she had to her identical twin and her willingness to commit fratricide in some act of vengeance. Not to mention, turning her jealous rage on Mark's girlfriend, Liann Nahuina, and four other women who had the misfortune of looking like Liann." His jaw set as he gazed at Elena. "Make that five women. Thankfully, one was able to survive." Logan sighed gratefully.

"We were both blessed in that way," she uttered, knowing it could just as easily have gone in the other direction and left him without the love he deserved in a partner.

"Yep." Logan released her hand and wrapped his long arm around Elena's shoulders protectively as they continued to walk on the beach. "Everything I said about Marlene Teale's mental fitness to go to trial could just as easily work against her as someone who was obviously cognizant and calculating enough to commit a string of blunt-force-trauma homicides and keep the authorities at bay for as long as she did. The good thing is that whichever way this goes, Teale's not likely to ever see the light of day again in the free world."

"Amen to that." The thought was comforting to Elena, for herself as a victim and in memory of those who didn't make it. Not to mention other Hawaiian women who might have been unjustly targeted for death by the unstable and evil serial killer. Elena lifted her chin and kissed Logan heartily, then, with romance on her mind, said, "Let's go home."

"If you insist," he said, grinning from ear to ear.

"Oh, yes," she assured him passionately, taking a peek at the two-tone gold wedding band on her finger, with its shimmering diamonds, that cemented their love. "I do."

* * * * *

R. Barri Flowers's miniseries, Hawaii CI, continues next month with Captured on Kauai. *You'll find it wherever Harlequin Intrigue books are sold!*

#2097 COWBOY JUSTICE AT WHISKEY GULCH
The Outriders Series • by Elle James
Outrider security agent Parker Shaw and his trusted equine and canine sidekicks are dedicated to safeguarding those in need. Having escaped abduction and imprisonment, Abby Gibson is hell-bent on rescuing the other captives. Trusting Parker is her only option. As danger nears, their choice may come down to saving themselves...or risking everything to save the hostages.

#2098 THE LOST HART TRIPLET
Covert Cowboy Soldiers • by Nicole Helm
Zara Hart is desperate to save her innocent sister and needs the help of her ranch's new owner. Undercover navy SEAL Jake Thompson knows he can't get involved in a murder case. But he *won't* let Zara lose her life searching for justice.

#2099 DEAD ON ARRIVAL
Defenders of Battle Mountain • by Nichole Severn
After barely escaping a deadly explosion, Officer Alma Majors has one clue to identify the victim and solve the case: a sliver of bone. But it's going to take more to expose the culprit. Bomb expert Cree Gregson will risk everything to protect his neighbor. Protecting his heart may prove more difficult...

#2100 MONTANA WILDERNESS PURSUIT
STEALTH: Shadow Team • by Danica Winters
Game warden Amber Daniels is tracking a bear on AJ Spade's ranch when he finds a hand wearing a sapphire ring—one he recognizes. A desperate rescue mission makes them learn to trust each other. Now they must work together to save themselves *and* a missing child.

#2101 CAPTURED ON KAUAI
Hawaii CI • by R. Barri Flowers
To discover why a fellow DEA agent was murdered, Dex Adair and his K-9 are undercover at Kauai's most beautiful resort. And when its owner, Katrina Sizemore, receives threatening letters, Dex suspects her husband's recent death might be connected. Is there a conspiracy brewing that will put a stop to Dex and Katrina's irresistible passion—forever?

#2102 ESCAPE FROM ICE MOUNTAIN
by Cassie Miles
When Jordan Reese-Waltham discovers her ex-husband's web of deceit, she must rescue her beloved twin sons. Her destination: ex-lover Blake Delaney's remote mountain retreat. The last thing she expects is for the former marine to appear. But with enemies on their trail, Jordan's reunion with Blake may end as soon as it begins...

SPECIAL EXCERPT FROM

ⒽHARLEQUIN

INTRIGUE

Join New York Times *bestselling author Elle James for the exciting conclusion of The Outriders series. Read on for a sneak peek at* Cowboy Justice at Whiskey Gulch.

Parker pulled his truck and horse trailer to a stop at the side of the ranch house and shifted into Park. Tired, sore from sitting for so long on the three-day trip from Virginia to Whiskey Gulch, Texas, he dreaded stepping out of the truck. When he'd stopped the day before, his leg had given him hell. Hopefully, it wouldn't this time.

Not in front of his old friend and new boss. He could show no weakness.

A nervous whine reminded him that Brutus needed to stretch as well. It had been several hours since their last rest stop. The sleek silver pit bull stood in the passenger seat, his entire body wagging since he didn't have a tail to do the job.

Parker opened the door and slid to the ground, careful to hold on to the door until he was sure his leg wasn't going to buckle.

It held and he opened the door wider.

"Brutus, come," he commanded.

Brutus leaped across the console and stood in the driver's seat, his mouth open, tongue lolling, happy to be there. Happy to be anywhere Parker was.

Ever since Parker had rescued the dog from his previous owner, Brutus had been glued to his side, a constant companion and eager to please him in every way.

Parker wasn't sure who'd rescued who. When he'd found Brutus tied to that tree outside a run-down mobile home starving, without water and in the heat of the summer, he'd known he couldn't leave the animal. He'd stopped his truck, climbed down and limped toward the dog, hoping he wouldn't turn on him and rip him apart.

Brutus had hunkered low to the ground, his head down, his eyes wary. He had scars on his face and body, probably from being beaten. A couple of the scars were round like someone had pressed a lit cigarette into his skin.

Parker had been sick to find the dog so abused. He unclipped the chain from Brutus's neck. Holding on to his collar, he limped with the dog back to the truck.

Brutus's previous owner had yelled from the door. "Hey! Thass my dog!"

Parker helped Brutus into the truck. The animal could barely make it up. He was too light for his breed, all skin and bone.

The owner came down from the trailer and stalked toward Parker barefoot, wearing a dirty, sleeveless shirt and equally dirty, worn jeans.

Parker had shut the truck door and faced the man.

The guy reeked of alcohol as he stopped in front of Parker and pointed at the truck. "I said, thass my dog!"

"Not anymore." Parker leveled a hard look at the man. "He's coming with me."

"The hell he is!" The drunk had lunged for the door.

Parker grabbed his arm, yanked it hard and twisted it up between the man's shoulder blades.

HIEXP0822